Dead Statues

(Kiera Hudson Series Two)
Book Four

Tim O'Rourke

Story Editor
Lynda O'Rourke
Book cover designed by:
Carles Barrios
Editor
Carolyn M. Pinard

This book is dedicated to the following people:

Lindy Roberts , Kerry Greenstreet , Jennifer Wilbourn , Olivia Finkova , Sally Cannell , Heather Allen Gunter , Tammy Middleton , Kerri Kitterman, Holly Harper , Lisa Ammari , Jennifer Bryson , Nichole Leonard , Arista McKim , Allyson Esmonde , Kerri Kitterman , Penny McCoy , Courtney Jackson , Stacey Hoy , Dawn Keagle , Tracie Wilson MacGregor , Mona Chavez-Bolanos , Kerry Anne Porter , Becky Lees , Gayle Morell , Toni 'bob' Francis, Mandy Foster-Meier , Louise Chapman , Melissa Wright , Jemma Wood , Rosie Dargue , Kiera Rose Hayles , Jen Montgomery, Tara Taggart , Stacey Crazymoo Szita , Tanya Bobrucki , Claire White , Amber Mundwiller , Emma Rapley , Georgia Leigh Stewart , Maria Vargas , Barbara Grubb , LeKeisha Kbaby Thomas , Louise Pearson , Jennifer Martin-Green, Sandra Litz , Jane Barron , Caroline Allison, Jane van der Merwe , Shelly Johnson, Kay Mcguinness , Hannah Landsburgh , Louise Kemp, Ann Garnett , Louise McGrath , Sharra Courter Turner , Jemma Wood , Emma Wilson , Kina Campbell , Amanda Porter, Heaven-Lei Taylor, Lieann Stonebank, Nereid Gwilliams

More books by Tim O'Rourke

Vampire Shift (Kiera Hudson Series 1) Book 1
Vampire Wake (Kiera Hudson Series 1) Book 2
Vampire Hunt (Kiera Hudson Series 1) Book 3
Vampire Breed (Kiera Hudson Series 1) Book 4
Wolf House (Kiera Hudson Series 1) Book 4.5
Vampire Hollows (Kiera Hudson Series 1) Book 5
Dead Flesh (Kiera Hudson Series 2) Book 1
Dead Night (Kiera Hudson Series 2) Book 1.5
Dead Angels (Kiera Hudson Series 2) Book 2
Dead Statues (Kiera Hudson Series 2) Book 3
Dead Seth (Kiera Hudson Series 2) Book 4
Dead Wolf (Kiera Hudson Series 2) Book 5
Dead Water (Kiera Hudson Series 2) Book 6
Witch (A Sydney Hart Novel)
Black Hill Farm (Book 1)
Black Hill Farm: Andy's Diary (Book 2)
Moonlight (Moon Trilogy) Book 1
Moonbeam (Moon Trilogy) Book 2
Vampire Seeker (Samantha Carter Series) Book 1

Author's Note:

This is the tenth Kiera Hudson book I have written. It has been quite some journey, not only for Kiera and her friends, but I guess for you, the reader, as well. So if you're reading this, I firstly wanted to take the time to say thank-you for coming this far on Kiera's journey.

'Dead Statues' isn't the longest book in either of the Kiera Hudson series', but it is probably the darkest and most emotional, as our heroine heads deeper into the world that has been *pushed*.

This book is split from both Kiera's and Potter's points of view and this is the first time this had happened in either series. There have been two short novels concerning Potter. The first is *'Wolf House'*, told solely from Potter's point of view, and the second, *'Dead Night'* told from both Potter's and Sophie's points of view. These two books were never intended as separate spinoff books from either Kiera Hudson series, but both of them have important characters and key plot developments which are crucial to the overall enjoyment and understanding of the book you are now holding in your hands, along with the rest of the series.

In both *'Wolf House'* and *'Dead Night'* Potter has kept secrets which are uncovered in *'Dead Statues.'* If you have followed Kiera's adventures this far but haven't read either *'Wolf House'* or *'Dead Night'*, you might want to visit those two stories first to really enjoy and understand *'Dead Statues.'*

It's up to you – and as Jack Seth might say, "You choose."

Whatever you decide, thank you so much for coming this far with Kiera Hudson, both of us truly appreciate it.

Take care,

Tim O'Rourke

Chapter One

Kiera

Push! That one word kept racing around my head, kicking up flaky fragments of brain matter and scattering them to the furthest corners of my mind. Potter sat slouched against the side of the wagon, his chin resting against his chest as he slept. The train tilted and shook as it snaked its way through the hills and down into the valleys. Kayla slept in the far corner of the wagon, dirty tear tracks down both of her cheeks. Sam lay beside her, half boy – half wolf. He seemed less restless than before, only stirring as the train lurched over points in the tracks.

I looked down at the picture in my hands. My dad stared out of it at me, he was smiling and his eyes were bright. He had one arm looped about my shoulder, and my head was tilted to one side, resting against his shoulder. As I stared at the picture in the weak shaft of moonlight that cut through the gap in the carriage door, I could see that I wasn't smiling. I looked surprised – confused, somehow. Before Potter had fallen asleep, I had told him that the photograph had yet to be taken. He hadn't believed me. I knew I was right, like Isidor had been right about the picture of him and Melody Rose. The photo of them had yet to be taken. Where had that beautiful picture of them standing together, looking happy, been snapped? Not in this world – not in the one which had been *pushed*. Isidor was dead now. I had seen it happen with my own eyes and I knew those images of him being decapitated by those Skin-walkers would never leave me. I looked up from the picture in my hands and stared at Kayla. How was she going to survive now without her brother by her side? How were any of us going to survive without Isidor? He was part of us – part of what I now thought of as my family. We had lost too many already. We had lost Murphy and he had left a gaping wound in Potter. I could see the pain every time I looked into his eyes – but just recently, I had seen something else there. It was like Potter knew more than he was telling me – not trusting in me. Why did I think that? I couldn't be sure. Since returning to Hallowed Manor from visiting my flat with the picture of me and my dad, Potter had been different. He had been distant from me. Perhaps *withdrawn* was the word I was searching for. When I'd shown him the word *PUSH* scrawled on the back of the picture, just like it had been written on the back of the photo of Isidor's, Potter had got that look in his eyes again. I had *seen* it. At the suggestion that my father might still be alive and that I would see him again, because how else had the picture ever been taken...Potter had become dismissive again. He had skulked away, where he propped himself against the side of the carriage and finally fell asleep.

"But I'm right about the picture," I whispered aloud, as if trying to convince myself. "I know I am."

The train rattled at speed over the tracks, and sliding the side door of the carriage open just an inch more, I peered down at the picture. What could I *see*? There must be something which would prove to me – to Potter – that the picture had yet to be taken, and had been put within my reach to lead me to my father. I held it up towards the gap in the door where the moonlight and chill night breeze rushed in. With my eyes screwed almost shut, I peered at the picture, trying to see anything – any clue as to where the picture might have been taken. The problem was, my father and I took up most of the picture, and what little I could see behind us was cast in gloomy shadow. It was impossible; I couldn't see where the picture had been taken.

Then, as a gust of freezing cold air tried to snatch the picture from my hand, I whispered, "Kiera, how can you be so dumb?" With my free hand, I raked away my long, black hair which blew about my face, and looked at the picture again. "It's not important where the picture was taken, but who took the photo – that's what matters!"

Realising I had been talking out loud, I glanced quickly about the carriage at the others. They were still asleep, so I looked once again back at the photograph. Someone must have taken the picture, right? Someone must have been there when I met up with my father again. Perhaps it might be this someone who would lead me to him? Then with my skin breaking out in gooseflesh, I lowered the picture and stared out through the gap in the door.

"Perhaps my mother took the picture?" I gasped.

If my dad was still alive in this *pushed* world, maybe my mother was too. But she was a Vampyrus, right? The Vampyrus had all been taken back below into The Hollows, and the tunnels had been sealed. There were no Vampyrus in this new world. Then slowly, I turned my head and looked at Potter as he sat hunched asleep against the side of the wagon. I knew that there was at least one.

Chapter Two

Potter

"Just keep away from me," I told her again, shifting my position against the tree so I didn't have to look at her. I didn't want to be close to her. Something deep inside of me was telling me it was wrong to be near her. Not because she was a threat to me, but because it wasn't Kiera.

Then I felt her hand gently squeeze my shoulder as she turned me around to face her. She looked into my eyes and said, "What's wrong?"

"I just want to be left alone," I whispered.

"That's no fun," she smiled.

"I haven't come here to have fun," I told her. "I've come to catch a killer." I looked over her shoulder and I could see I was back at the wolf house. Even now I felt the dread and the pain seeping from its ram-shackled frame. In the distance, I could hear the faint sound of children sobbing for their mothers.

Leaning in close to me, she whispered, "Something is happening here –"

"I know, children are being murdered…" I started.

"No, I didn't mean that," she whispered, brushing herself close against me. "Something is happening between you and me – you feel it too, I know you do."

I did feel it. The feelings I had for Eloisa Madison were wrong. I shouldn't be feeling like this for anyone other than Kiera. My head was telling me that it was okay. Eloisa Madison was before I'd met Kiera. Eloisa had happened after Sophie. So that was okay, wasn't it?

"I don't know what you're talking about," I lied as she looked into my eyes, her lips hovering over mine.

"I've never met a man like you before, Potter," she whispered, "a man who has such a dark side. You could take me away from all of this."

"From all of what?" I said, fighting the desire to kiss her.

"All this death," she whispered, then pressed her lips against mine.

As if drowning, I felt smothered by a wave of intense feelings and emotions, like nothing I had felt before, and I was kissing her back. Her tongue felt like velvet in my mouth as she hungrily pulled at me. Then I was falling backwards as she pushed me down onto the ground. I fell onto the carpet of leaves and pine needles that covered the floor of the woods. She sprang on top of me, pulling open my coat and nipping the skin of my neck with her teeth. The trees seemed to close in all around us, shielding us from view, like we were in our own world.

Eloisa's soft hair fell across my face, and it felt so good. I ran my hands down her back and scratched at her with my claws. Leaning up, she threw aside her shirt, and the chain with the cross shone just inches from my face.

Murphy's chain?

Kiera's chain!

Eloisa Madison lowered herself onto me and her skin felt warm and soft. I entwined my fingers in her hair and stared up into her eyes, but Madison had gone. It was Kiera I was making love to. I rolled her over onto the soft cushion of leaves and her breath felt hot against my neck as she said, "I love you, Potter."

To hear her voice made my heart race as it was filled with joy. I made love to her and it felt like nothing I had experienced with her before. Although my heart was telling me it was Kiera, my head was telling me it was someone else. As I opened my eyes and looked down upon her face, it was Eloisa I could hear moaning and sighing softly beneath me.

"No!" I murmured, trying to pull myself free of her.

15

I arched my back and looked up. It was somehow colder now. A thin wisp of fog covered the ground. In it I could see a figure staring back at me from between the trees.

"Kiera?" I called out. "Is that you?" my heart raced, fearing that it was. Had she seen me with Eloisa? Had she seen what we had done?

I glanced back down, but Eloisa Madison had gone. There was only me on my knees, bent double in the damp autumn leaves.

"Potter," someone whispered, and I knew it was the person watching from between the trees who had spoken.

I looked up to see Murphy, standing in a swirl of fog like some unholy apparition.

"I've got something to show you," he barked from around his pipe which jutted from the corner of his mouth. "Stop pricking about in the dirt and get over here!"

I clambered to my feet, and without saying another word and keeping close to the trees, Murphy led me towards a small graveyard. We hadn't gone very far when he flapped his hand at me, signalling me to get down. I crouched behind a gravestone that tilted slightly to the right and peered over the top.

"What am I meant to be looking at?" I whispered to Murphy, who was hiding behind a gravestone to my left.

With the pipe hanging from the corner of his mouth, Murphy pointed into the distance. From my hiding place, I looked in the direction he was pointing and saw a man standing alone in the middle of the graveyard. He was staring down at one of the headstones. It was as I looked at his drawn and ashen face that I recognised him, and my stomach knotted. The man I was spying on was Kiera's father. Hadn't he died of cancer a few years back? I wondered.

I shot a look at Murphy, but it was if he had melted away like a ghost. "Kiera's father is still very much alive here," he whispered.

With his head cast down, Kiera's father turned and seemed to slowly float back across the graveyard and disappear. When he had gone, Murphy stood up and rubbed the small of his back with his hands.

"C'mon," he whispered, his voice sounding as if it were coming from miles away.

I set off after him. Murphy stood before a headstone, and not wanting to look at the name carved into the face of it, I stared at the flowers that Kiera's father had left behind. Some of the petals broke loose in the wind and scattered over the grave like confetti.

"Look at the grave," Murphy whispered.

"I am," I said.

"Look at the name."

"I can't."

"You have to," his voice changing from a whisper to a scream.

Lowering my eyes, I looked down at the headstone and read the name written across it: Kiera Hudson. It made me feel sick to look at her name, and although I knew Kiera was dead here – she wasn't to me; she was still very much alive.

"Kiera will want to see her father – she loves him – she made him a promise..." I breathed, looking sideways through the fog at my friend.

"No!" Murphy snapped. "She must never find out that her father is still alive here. If she does, then like you say, she will want to see him, speak with him, it would only be natural. But she can't. Our Kiera is not his Kiiiiiieeeeeraaa," his voice trailed away.

"They come from two different whens," I said, trying to make sense of everything, my mind seeming to be filled with as much fog as the graveyard.

"Exactly," Murphy hushed, now suddenly standing in front of me. "What if Kiera were to meet her father? Would she then want to push the world back and lose him all over again?" He stared into my eyes, pipe smoke smelling like rotten flesh.

"But I can't keep a secret like that from her," I whispered back. "She has a right to know that her father is still alive."

"She has no rights!" Murphy grimaced, his face contorting out of shape like a nightmarish Halloween mask. "She doesn't have the right to be here – none of us do. Kiera's father believes his daughter is dead, and she is as far as this world is concerned. What would happen if he knew that she was living again on the other side of the country? It's not her – it's not the Kiera that you are in love with; it's the Kiera who was brought up in a world where wolves live amongst humans. It's a world where she is dead."

"I don't know if I can keep something like this from her," I said.

"You must keep her away from her old life, Potter," Murphy said, his voice now sounding like Isidor's, as if he were somehow warning me from beyond the grave. "If her father should see her, then perhaps the world will merge just a little bit more, then a little bit more, and I fear that could be catastrophic for all of us."

"But I don't want to keep secrets from my friends, especially not from Kiera," I shuddered. "She would hate me if she found out that her father was still alive and I hadn't told her."

"Then you better make sure that she never finds out about her father," Murphy said in his own voice again, with a grim smile on his face. Then added, "Or about your friend, Sophie."

I looked away in shame, even though nothing had happened between me and Sophie – not in this when. She had tempted me, but I had been true to Kiera. It was Kiera who I loved. I could never hurt her.

"So?"

"So what?" I asked, looking back at Murphy. But he had gone, and so had the fog and the graveyard. I was standing in a bedroom and Sophie appeared naked before me. I half expected her to cover her breasts with her arms and yell at me to get out, but she didn't, she just stood there, her head to one side, looking at me. One side of her face looked broken and battered as if she had been hit by a car.

"What do you want?" she asked me.

"Do you want me to leave?" I said.

"No," she whispered, and the room suddenly flickered with candlelight. "Do you want to leave?"

"No," I said, closing the door behind me.

Sophie came towards me, and as she did, I felt a thumping sensation race through my body. It was like a ghost of a heart, racing inside of me. She stopped and her neck made a sickening crunching sound as if snapping back into place. We were so close that I could see she was trembling. "I do remember you," she whispered. "I remember everything. I remember how much I loved you and I know how much I hurt you."

"How do you know?" I whispered back.

"The letters you sent me," she said, her eyes looking into mine. "They were full of pain."

"I'm not hurting anymore," I said.

"Are you sure?" she asked as she folded her arms about me. They felt stiff and cold and her skin smelt as if she was decomposing, in my arms.

"I'm sure," I said, closing my eyes. "I'm in love with another."

Sophie seemed to flinch in my arms and pull slightly away from me. "Kiera Hudson?" she breathed and the bones in her broken neck made that crunching sound again.

"Yes," I told her. "I love her more than anything."

"But you loved me," she frowned.

I opened my eyes to see that she was staring into them again, and the hurt that I could see there was almost unbearable. I had loved Sophie once, and those feelings which I thought had been snuffed out like a flame, slowly rekindled themselves inside of me. She had been my first love.

"That was a long time ago, in another where and another when," I whispered, wanting to run from her.

"What about what we shared?" she suddenly screamed, pulling me close again. "What about us?"

Then instead of pushing her away like I had done in the cottage, high on Black Hill, I pulled her close. Her naked body now felt soft and warm against mine. The touch of her hair against my cheek made my phantom heart race. My mind told me it raced not from lust or desire, but out of fear. I wanted to push Sophie away – she wasn't Kiera. It was Kiera I wanted to be holding naked against me. It was Kiera who I wanted to be lowering onto the bed in the glow of the warm candlelight. Sophie smiled up at me, only the whites of her eyes showing. She raised her arms, her breasts just inches from my face. They looked wrinkled and old, like two withered balloons. With my eyes closed, and searching for Kiera in my mind, I heard her voice. It was soft at first – like a whisper.

"No!"

Then louder.

"No! Potter!"

Louder still. Almost a scream.

"No! Potter...

"...Potter!" Kiera cried out.

I opened my eyes. Kiera was standing by the carriage door which was now open. Wind blew her long, dark hair about her face and shoulders. With my dream breaking apart into tiny fragments, I stumbled to my feet and went to her. I felt sick with guilt, even though I had only been dreaming. Sophie and Eloisa hadn't been real – they had just come back to haunt me. Just as Murphy had. All of them had come back to remind me I was keeping secrets from the woman I loved.

"What's wrong?" I said over the roar of the passing wind which buffeted the side of the train.

"The picture!" Kiera cried.

"Picture?" I frowned, the last remaining shards of my nightmare blinding me.

"The picture of me and my dad," she said, leaning out of the open carriage and back along the tracks. "It flew out of the door."

"How?" I asked, scratching my head, still feeling a little groggy.

"I don't know!" Kiera snapped. "It was like it was snatched out of my hand somehow. Taken away from me."

I looked at her, tears standing in the corners of her eyes. It hurt me to see the pain she felt at losing that picture of her dad. However much I hated it myself, I also felt relieved, too. Perhaps now, without the picture as a constant reminder, Kiera's desire to go looking for her father might lessen. Deep inside of me, I doubted that. Had I been able to stop myself looking for Sophie? No. However much I told myself I had gone in search of Sophie to try and find out if she knew why the world had been *pushed*, I knew that was just a bunch of crap. That's why I had dreamt of her. She hadn't come back to haunt my dreams, my guilt had. That's what was eating me up inside.

21

I looked at Kiera standing by the open carriage door as she peered back along the track for any sign of that picture, which had meant so much to her. The pain in her eyes told me she was going to go in search of her father – picture or no picture. Now I'm not known for my sensitive side, but to see that look of desperation in her eyes – panic – crushed me, and I just wanted to tell her everything. I didn't want to keep those fucking secrets that Murphy had crapped on me from such a great height. I wanted to be honest with Kiera, I owed her that. She should know that her father was still alive, that cancer hadn't eaten him like it had before the world had been *pushed*. Didn't she have a right to know?

"She has no rights!" Murphy whispered in my ear. *"She doesn't have the right to be here – none of us do."*

What would Kiera think of me if I told her now? What would she think of me if she knew I had met Murphy again during those twenty-four hours that I had been away from Hallowed Manor? She'd want to know why I hadn't told her that Murphy was alive, and why I had kept it a secret from her. Worse still, Kiera would want to know why I hadn't told her about her dad.

I moved slowly towards her, and taking her in my arms, she rested her head against my chest. "I'm sorry," I whispered.

"It's not your fault," she said, thinking I was talking about the picture.

As I held her close in my arms, I felt the train begin to slow. I didn't want it to stop just yet, I wanted to keep moving so I could stay and hold her close to me. Then, looking over her shoulder I watched the night sky as it flashed with pulses of luminous blue light. The Skin-walkers disguised as cops had caught up with us, and the train was slowing so they could greet us.

Chapter Three

Kiera

"We've got company," Potter whispered in my ear.

"Huh?" I breathed, pulling away from him.

"Skin-walkers," he snapped, stretching out his fingers and setting his claws free like a row of knives. "Wake the others."

I looked back out of the carriage door as the train came to a juddering halt. A plume of thick, black diesel smoke belched from the engine and up into the dawn sky. The train had stopped at a level crossing, and on either side of the road, police vehicles were parked with their emergency lights flashing red and blue like streaks of lightning. Some of the Skin-walkers, dressed as cops, had left their vehicles and were now walking alongside the tracks and checking the train for us. Cones of torchlight splashed the sides of the train, and I could hear the sounds of their boots crunching over the ballast.

Slowly, I eased the carriage door shut. Then, turning on the heels of my boots, I darted across to the wagon. I shook Kayla gently by the shoulder, and whispered, "Wake up."

Kayla stirred and I shook her again. She opened her eyes and looked up at me. Before she'd had the chance to say anything, I gently placed my hand over her mouth.

"Shhh. Skin-walkers are searching the train," I told her.

Brushing my hand aside, Kayla pulled herself up, and producing her claws as quickly as Potter had, she looked at me and said, "Good. I want to mess with those fuckers for what they did to Isidor."

"That's my girl," Potter smirked, then kicked Sam in the ribs with his boot. "Rise and shine, Teen-Wolf. It's time you proved which side you're on."

Sam howled in pain and threw his hands to his sides.

"Nice one!" I glared at Potter. "Why don't you just stick a big neon sign above the carriage saying 'We are here'?"

"I hardly touched him," Potter said. Then looking down at Sam, he added, "You'd better man-up or wolf-out, boy, because some of your furry friends are getting ready to tear us all a new set of arseholes!"

Sam pulled himself up as Kayla took his arm to support him. Unlike the other Skin-walkers, who looked either human or werewolf when changed, Sam looked stuck somewhere in between. Long, thick lengths of dark brown hair hung from his head, his cheeks, and chin. His eyes glowed yellow, and his teeth were jagged and sharp-looking in his mouth. His long arms swung down by his sides, and I could see that just like the rest of him, they were covered in thick, dark brown, bristly hair. Each of his fingers was capped with ivory-looking nails that were sharp and pointed.

"Are you okay?" I asked him.

"Fine," he said, glaring at Potter.

"You shouldn't have kicked him like that," Kayla hissed.

"He's one of them," Potter snapped back.

"No, he's not," Kayla shot.

"Really?" Potter barked. Then turning his attention back at Sam, he added. "Did you sue him?"

"Sue who?" Sam asked confused.

"Your fucking hairdresser," Potter grinned rolling up his sleeves, readying himself for the Skin-walkers who were growing ever nearer. "If I came out looking like you with hair and shit sprouting outta me, I'd be demanding a refund."

"That's not funny!" Kayla cut in, defending her friend.

"Good," Potter snapped at her, "because I wasn't trying to be amusing. All I'm trying to say is, once a wolf always a wolf.

Just because he looks semi-human, doesn't make him one. However hard you try Kayla, you can't polish a turd."

"I'm not a piece of shit!" Sam barked at him, his eyes glowing fiercely.

"Glad to hear it," Potter smiled at him. "Because now you're gonna get a chance to prove it." No sooner had the words left his mouth then Potter had yanked aside the carriage door. As if surprised to see Potter there, the Skin-walkers outside glanced up at him and roared.

With their hands turning into claws, the Skin-walkers ripped their police uniforms from their bodies and threw themselves at the side of the train. As they leapt through the air, their human forms took on the shape of giant wolves. One moment their bodies were pale, almost undernourished-looking, and in the next, they were rippling with muscle, covered in coats of shiny, black fur, their heads like that of giant wolves with gaping jaws.

As the wolves leapt at Potter, he glanced at me, and with a smile tugging at the corner of his lips, he whispered, "What you waiting for, sweet-cheeks?"

Then he was gone, throwing himself free of the carriage, and clattering into the wolves.

Chapter Four

Potter

I don't know why, but tearing up wolves made me smile. I'm not sure whether it was the thrill of it, or if there wasn't just a little part of me that enjoyed the killing. After all, I was a Vampyrus, and you couldn't polish a turd, right? With a grin that I guess made me look a little crazy, I sprang from the side of the train carriage, driving my right claw into the foaming snout of one of the Skin-walkers, my left slicing away the head of another. Their blood splattered up my forearms in hot, sticky streams and I knew I had stepped over that line again. The line which separated my human side to that of my darker – Vampyrus – side. My wings shifted beneath the flesh that covered my back, eager to be set free. If I released them, I would have to kill every single one of these motherfuckers. I couldn't risk one of them reporting back what they had seen. As the Skin-walkers flew away in strips of fur and flesh, I thought of Isidor standing alone in the railway station waiting room as those Skin-walkers crept up on him from behind. In my mind I could see them attack and kill my friend. As I relived the moment Isidor's head split from his neck and flew wide-eyed across the waiting room, I knew that I had no intention of letting one of these sorry-looking arseholes live. So with a shrug of my shoulders, I felt my coat tear open along my spine. My skin made a cracking sound as my wings unfolded from within me, and my mouth gushed with blood as my fangs slid from my gums. With my wings beating furiously on either side of me, two of the Skin-walkers, who were now racing towards me along the tracks, faltered. They looked at one another as if unable to believe what it was they were seeing.

"That's right, you pathetic bitches in heat," I roared at them. "You didn't really think I would let you kill my friend and just walk away, did you?"

The Skin-walkers, in their finely-pressed police uniforms, looked at each other again, then back at me. My long, black wings trailed in the ballast as I walked slowly towards them. Their human faces still looked shocked, as if I had slapped them already. I flexed open my claws, blood flying from them. Then one of the cops snatched his radio from his belt.

"Release the berserkers!" he roared.

Before he'd had the chance to fix his radio back in place, the air was filled with the most ear-piercing screech I had ever heard. In a streak of black shadows, the cop was snatched up into the air. As he rocketed upwards, he clawed frantically at his uniform as he changed form. Momentarily wondering if in fact these Skin-walkers could actually fly themselves, I saw the black shadow which flickered all around him take shape. Kayla came into view, and I could see that she had sunk her claws into the chest of the Skin-walker that now dangled beneath her as she hovered high up. Her wings glistened in the light of the rising sun, and the glittery-like substance which covered them shone red and pink. Her hair billowed out behind her like flames, as she threw her head forward and sunk her face into the creature's chest. In one swift movement, she yanked her head back and I could see Kayla had something round and black hanging from her mouth, and it beat rapidly in and out. With thick streams of blood swinging from her chin, she snatched the Skin-walker's heart from between her jaws and rammed it into the creature's mouth.

"That's for Isidor," she screeched, then tossed the dead Skin-walker away through the air.

Distracted by Kayla, I hadn't noticed the other cop tear away its flesh and transform into the giant wolf, which was now leaping through the air towards me. I thrust my claws out before me, but there was no need. The wolf suddenly flew backwards through the air in a mass of flowing hair and fur. Sam howled as he bounded into the Skin-walker. With his arms working like pistons, he lunged, ripped, and clawed at the Skin-walker as they flew through the air. The Skin-walker fought back, as it snapped its mighty jaws just inches from Sam's face. With a roar so loud it sounded like an express train racing through a tunnel, Sam went berserk. With ferocity I had only seen my friend Murphy capable of, Sam gutted, then shredded the Skin-walker in a blaze of flashing claws and teeth.

In the distance I could see more flashing blue lights approaching. The group of Skin-walkers, who had arrived in the first wave of emergency vehicles, were now racing along the tracks towards us. They bounded forward on all fours, tearing away their uniforms as they changed in a blinding flash of muscle and fur. They were huge, like giant bears, and their pointed paws threw up great plumes of ballast and chalky white dust. Two of them leapt at the side of the train and I glanced up to see what had drawn their attention. In one swift bound, they had both landed on the roof of the train, where Kiera was running along the top of it. Like my own, her wings were out. Both were angled upwards, and the claws at each tip snatched at the air. Her thick, black hair trailed out behind her, and as always in her half-breed form, it shone blue in thick silky streaks. Her beautiful face looked pale in the weak winter sunlight which was now shining over the tops of the mountain peaks in the distance. I watched Kiera race along the roof of the train as the Skin-walker bounded towards her. With my own wings thrumming on either side of me, I leapt into the air and soared towards her. The cold air blew my hair from my face, and I knew that however hard I pushed myself forward, I wouldn't reach Kiera before the wolves were upon her. Then, just as the wolves swiped at her with their massive hooked claws, Kiera flipped through the air, dragging her long, bladed fingernails down the lengths of their backs. The creatures howled and span around, screaming over the roof of the train as they fought to hold on. As they turned, the long, ragged gashes Kiera had opened down the lengths of their backs popped open like a bulging seam, spilling their innards and entrails from them. As I swooped in towards Kiera, I saw one of the wolves collapse onto its side, his huge jaws open as it lay panting, desperately sucking in his last mouthful of air. The other seemed not to know what had happened to it, and the wolf took two more giant bounds back towards Kiera before its paws got entangled in its own entrails. The wolf made a yelping sound as it slipped and tripped on its own guts. Making a gargling sound in the back of its throat, the wolf fell from the roof of the carriage, but its intestines had become ensnared and the creature swung like a giant blood-red pendulum alongside the train.

I landed on the roof next to Kiera, her claws dripping red by her sides. The hazel colour of her eyes glowed almost orange and I couldn't help but notice the faintest of cracks appearing around her eyes and the corners of her mouth. As if reading my mind, Kiera licked the blood from her claws and almost at once, those tiny cracks faded away.

"Are you okay?" I asked her.

"For now," she said, glancing back over her shoulder at the police vehicles which were now screaming to a halt at the level crossing. The dawn sky pulsated blue and red as the emergency vehicles made the *Whoop! Whoop!* sound.

Kayla swept out of the sky and settled beside us, as Sam bounded up from the tracks. His claws made a clacking sound along the roof as he came leaping towards us.

"We can't just fly out of here," I said, withdrawing my wings into my back.

"Why not?" Kayla said, her own wings buzzing behind her.

I looked at her and had to stop myself from telling Kayla what Murphy had told me. His words went around in my head as I remembered what he had said.

The wolves have been waiting for hundreds of years for an angel to come, Murphy had explained. *All they know is that this angel with wings will be female and will be aided by four others. They believe that she will come and destroy the Treaty that exists between them and the humans and will eventually destroy the wolves. They don't know her name or when she will come. All they know is that this angel will be dead already.*

With Murphy's voice ringing in my ears, I looked at Kayla and said, "This world doesn't have human-looking creatures that have wings..." before I'd the chance to finish my lame excuse, one of the police vehicles' back doors was thrown open. At first I thought the low rumbling sound I could hear was thunder rolling in across the hills that surrounded us. The morning sky was clear; the storm clouds had long since passed. I looked at the police van again with its doors open and realised the sound was coming from within it. Slowly, the others turned to look back in the direction of the deep booming noise. We watched as the creatures climbed from the back of the police van. They looked like wolves, but they walked upright like men. Their giant paws swung against their knees, and each of them had wide open jaws which were lined with rows of jagged teeth. Their crimson eyes burnt bright within their colossal skulls. These were the creatures which had been sent to hunt us and kill Isidor, the humans – freaks – that had failed to be matched correctly with the wolves. They had been left deranged, wild, and crazed. They were half wolf-half human – neither species claiming responsibility for them.

"Berserkers," I whispered and looked at Sam.

Chapter Five

Kiera

I watched the creatures spill from the back of the police van. They sniffed the air with long, pointed snouts and made woofing sounds deep within their throats. Even the other Skin-walkers that were present seemed to shy away from them. Then from the back of the van climbed several other police officers. These were dressed from head to foot in thick, black, padded armour, like riot officers. Their faces were covered in masks, which had metal grills covering their features. It was then I noticed that each of these officers held what looked like reins in their gloved fists. The reins were attached to collars which circled the berserkers' scrawny throats. I had known several police dog handlers on the force back in the other world before it had got pushed. However, none of them had ever handled such wild and furious-looking beasts as the berserkers.

"There are too many of them," I said over my shoulder at the others. "If they set those things loose, then we're..."

Before I'd had the chance to finish what I was saying, the cops were leading the yapping and snarling berserkers along the tracks towards us like a pack of bloodhounds.

"Wings in!" Potter snapped.

"But..." Kayla started.

"We can't afford to let them see us like this," Potter barked, looking at me. I hadn't seen it often, but I could see fear in his eyes. I didn't believe it was in fear of the berserkers, but something else.

With the sound of the woofing and howling behind me, I glanced back to see the berserkers and the handlers racing along the tracks below us. The cops' radios crackled as frantic messages screeched out into the night. Then as one, the officers released the leashes on the berserkers and set them free. At an incredible speed, the berserkers raced forward. Within moments they were scampering and clawing their way up the side of the train carriages and bounding towards us.

"Run!" Potter roared, turning and racing away along the roof of the train.

"Run where?" I yelled after him.

Together we raced away, the sound of the berserkers' claws scratching at the roof of the train. I looked back and saw streams of drool, turned silver in the morning light, spray from their snarling jaws. Then, behind them, I saw one of the police vans break free from the others and come racing alongside the train. With emergency lights blazing and sirens screaming, the van raced towards us. Looking front, and fearing that it was filled with more of those terrifying berserkers, I sped up. Potter, Kayla, and Sam raced ahead of me, but we were fast running out of train. From the corner of my eye, I saw the police van draw level with us. It slowed, then, unable to believe what I was seeing, Murphy lent through the open window.

With his thick, white hair blowing back off his brow, and pipe dangling from the corner of his mouth, he roared up at us, "What are you waiting for, you fucking Muppets! Jump!"

Potter leapt from the train first, followed by Kayla and Sam. Still wondering if my eyes were deceiving me, but praying they weren't, I looked back once more as the berserkers lunged at me. Then I jumped. I landed on top of the police van as it bumped and listed over the ballast. Pieces of grey stone flew up from beneath the wheels of the van as it crunched over the tracks, and away from the train. Potter was punching his fist into the roof of the van. Then with his claws out, he made a circular motion, cutting a hole in the metal roof.

Then, peeling it back like a can of sardines, he looked up at Kayla and Sam and shouted, "Get inside!"

The van skidded to the right, and I flew sideways, the heels of my boots teetering on the edge of the van.

"Easy, tiger!" Potter snapped, taking hold of my hand and pulling me to safety.

The berserkers had leapt from the train and were now racing alongside the van. They snapped and clawed at the side of it, trying to hold on with their bony claws. In Potter's arms, I peered over the edge of the van to see one of the berserkers take hold of the handle on the driver's door. It flew open and again I saw the driver, who I thought looked like Murphy, as he nearly fell out of the speeding vehicle. Then lashing out with his leg, he drove his foot into the berserker's muzzle.

"Get away, you filthy mutt!" Murphy roared, as he drove his foot repeatedly into the upturned and snarling face of the berserker.

I wanted to believe it was Murphy – but somehow, I couldn't. The last time I had seen him was beneath the Fountain of Souls, where he had been betrayed by Jack Seth. Those images of him being fed to the wolves still haunted my nightmares. I glanced down again, still not believing what I was seeing. It wasn't the sound of his gruff voice, his thick shock of white hair, or even the waft of pipe smoke which finally convinced me that my friend was back from the dead – it was the sight of his slippered foot smashing repeatedly into the snout of the berserker. Murphy had been the only police officer I had ever known who carried out his duties while wearing a pair of carpet slippers.

"That's Murphy!" I squealed at Potter.

"I know," he said back.

"What do you mean you know?" I asked him.

"I can recognise my old sergeant when I see him," he said, guiding me to the hole he'd made in the roof.

"I thought you'd be..." I started.

"What?" he said, staring into my eyes.

"Pleased," I breathed. "I know how much you've missed him."

Potter looked away, but in that moment just before he did, I saw that look in his eyes – the one I couldn't quite describe, other than he was keeping something back from me.

"What's wrong?" I asked, taking him by the arm and forcing him to look at me.

"We need to talk," he said, then disappeared into the hole.

I climbed in behind him as the van rattled and shook. Behind the driver's seat there was room enough for a small unit of police officers. Kayla sat in one of the seats, her mouth open as she stared at Murphy. Sam sat beside her, staring back out of the window as we sped away from the berserkers and their handlers. The sound of the sirens above us was deafening. Potter climbed into the front seat next to Murphy. He said something to him, but I couldn't hear what it was he said. Everything was wrong with this picture, and I didn't need to be able to *see* things to know it.

Potter wasn't the kind of guy who showed his feelings that often, but I knew how much the death of Murphy had hurt him, so I at least expected him to look just a little surprised at Murphy rising from the dead. I looked at Potter and could see he looked more pissed off than happy at Murphy's return. Murphy glanced in the wing mirror, then at Potter.

"We're not out of trouble yet," Murphy barked. "We've got two police vehicles in pursuit."

Then, as if never being apart, Potter nodded at his old sergeant as if knowing exactly what to do. He scrambled out of his seat and came into the back of the vehicle where I sat watching him. Without making eye contact, he brushed past me. Holding onto the side of the van to keep himself from toppling over, Potter raised one leg and kicked open the rear doors. They flew apart and I could see the train way off in the distance. The berserkers were some way behind, and unable to keep up with us. Just like Murphy had warned, there were two police cruisers racing just inches from the back of the van. The driver of one of the vehicles lurched the police cruiser forward, its reinforced bumper ramming into the back of the van. We skidded sideways across the narrow country road we were now on.

"What are you waiting for, Potter? Fucking Christmas?" Murphy roared from up front.

Without saying anything, Potter threw me a sideways glance, and then flung himself from the back of the van. The windshield of the police vehicle shattered inwards as Potter collided with it. With his claws sprung open, Potter reached in through the broken glass, and in one swift movement, he yanked the driver from his seat and tossed him backwards out of the vehicle. I watched the cop hurtle through the air towards me. Ducking, the cop landed in the back of the van. After being momentarily stunned, he shook his head from side to side, and then started to change form. With his eyes blazing yellow, the transforming Skin-walker jumped to its feet. Murphy threw the van violently to the right. Fearing that the vehicle might just topple over, I dug my claws into the nearest seat and with my free hand, I swiped at the Skin-walker. It snarled and leapt away. Murphy swung the van to the left, throwing the Skin-walker back towards me. With my claws held out before me, the Skin-walker became impaled on them. My hand felt suddenly hot inside the creature, and it snapped its giant jaws just inches from my face. I clenched its innards in my fists, and twisted my arm to the right. The Skin-walker's burning eyes bulged in their sockets as it howled in pain. Then it collapsed on top of me, sending me sprawling to my arse. My head and shoulders hung out from the back of the van, the side of my face just inches from the ground. Long lengths of my hair brushed over the surface of the road and whipped around the wheels.

The dead Skin-walker was a crushing weight on top of me, and with my hand still trapped inside the creature, I couldn't lever it off me. Fearing that my hair would become entangled around the spinning wheels and drag me beneath them, I screamed for help. Sam and Kayla came to my rescue, heaving the giant wolf from me. My fist made a squelching sound as it came out from within the Skin-walker. With one swift kick, Kayla ejected the dead creature from the back of the police van. It rolled and bounced onto the road, where it disappeared beneath the wheels of the police car which Potter was now driving. Taking me by the arm, Sam pulled me to my feet.

"Are you okay?" he woofed.

"I guess," I said, looking back at Potter as he raced towards us. The police car which tailed him slammed into the back of his car, forcing him into the rear of our van.

Knowing that if I didn't act quickly Potter would be sandwiched between the two vehicles, I leapt from the back of the van. I ran over the bonnet of the police vehicle which Potter was fighting desperately to control. I clambered over the roof and the flashing emergency lights, and slid over the trunk and onto the bonnet of the police vehicle behind. With my hair fanning out behind me like blue streaks of lightning, I drove my fist into the windshield. Just like Kristy Hall had attacked my police cruiser back in the Ragged Cove all those months ago, I forced my head and shoulders through the broken windshield and lunged at the cop's face with my fangs. His flesh came away in thin slices as my fangs slid over the length of his skull. The cop threw his hands to his face, as his snout and whiskers appeared. With my phantom-like heart racing in my chest, I bit and tore at him. His skin fell away just like orange peel, but instead of revealing juicy segments of fruit, the face of a giant wolf appeared. It howled and bit back at me. The police car jack-knifed across the road, throwing me across the bonnet. I sunk my claws into the side of the car as the wolf burst through what was left of the windshield. With thick clouds of black smoke belching from the engine, I scrambled onto the bonnet of the car. The wolf spun round in search of me. Spying me in the glare of the pulsating emergency lights, the wolf sprung from the bonnet. Then the vehicle seemed to crumble as the wolf suddenly flew over me. I glanced down to see that Potter had thrown his own vehicle into reverse, smashing into us and throwing the wolf clear.

Only stunned, the wolf rolled onto all fours and came racing back down the centre of the road towards me. I crouched low on the top of the car with my fangs and claws at the ready. Then as the wolf leapt into the air, my wings shot out from within me and I flipped back through the air and over the wolf. It glanced up and howled as if wondering where I had suddenly vanished to. In that moment of confusion, I corkscrewed out of the sky and tore its head from its shoulders. The wolf's blood spattered my face, and my tongue licked it away from the corners of my mouth. I let go of its head and it dropped through the air like a stone. With my wings closing, I skimmed just inches above the road as I raced back towards Potter. The car he had been driving looked like it had just been pulled from the crusher, and he stood propped against the bonnet with a cigarette dangling from the corner of his mouth. His arms and face were covered in streaks of blood, as were mine.

In the distance I could see that Murphy had brought the van to a halt, and the brakes glowed red like two hot coals. He lent from the window and roared at us.

"When you two have quit screwing around, perhaps you would like to come and join us! There'll be more of those things heading our way."

I looked at Potter as he took the cigarette from his mouth and flicked it into the bushes. "Murphy's right, we should get going," he said.

Then, looking him straight in his blood-stained face, I said, "You knew he was alive, didn't you?"

"Yes," he said.

"So why didn't you tell me?" I asked, as Potter turned to walk away. I couldn't believe Potter could keep the fact that my friend was alive a secret. How long had he known Murphy was back from the dead? What had Murphy been doing and how long had he been back? More importantly, why had he only seen Potter and not me, Kayla and Isidor? Before Potter had gone a yard, I grabbed his arm and said, "What else haven't you told me? What other secrets have you been keeping from me?"

Murphy pressed on the horn as he leant from the window again. "C'mon!" he roared.

Potter made to move away and again I grabbed him. "What else haven't you told me?"

Then very slowly, Potter turned to look at me. With that look of fear – or was it sadness – in his eyes, he said, "Your father is alive, Kiera. I've seen him."

I stood and watched Potter walk back towards the police van. Even though my whole body felt bruised and battered from the attack we had just endured, it was nothing compared to the pain I felt inside, knowing that Potter had been keeping the truth about Murphy and my father from me.

Chapter Six

Potter

Murphy drove the van down across the narrow lanes with their tight curves and bends. There was no other traffic on the road. Vast fields spread out on either side of us, a thin layer of fog hovering like dry-ice over the long grass, the tips of the blades sparkling with dewdrops in the morning light. It was a beautiful morning, and the storm of the previous night had left a crisp winter breeze in its wake. The sky was dove-white, and I wondered if snow was coming.

I turned away from the window and glanced at Murphy. He had a grim look on his face as he stared at the road ahead. The atmosphere in the van was as frosty as the chill wind which buffeted the side of the van. I dared not glance back at the others – at Kiera – I knew she was watching me. I could feel her eyes boring into the back of my head like two pointed screwdrivers. Why had Murphy come back so suddenly? Why hadn't he sent me some kind of warning so I could figure out what I was going to say to Kiera? She saw most things at the best of times – but Murphy showing up like this was like pointing a giant finger at me. I couldn't act – I wasn't even a great liar. How the fuck had Murphy imagined I was going to keep something like this from Kiera? I should've never agreed to keep the secret about her father and Murphy coming back from the dead from her.

Murphy glanced at me and then looked away again. Could he see how pissed off I was? I wanted to ask him why. If I did, Kiera would hear me – they all would, and now wasn't the time. Not in the van. I needed to get my thoughts together, figure out exactly what I was going to tell Kiera. How much was I going to tell her? It wasn't only the secrets I had kept from her about

Murphy and her father – there was my secret meeting with Sophie, too. It wasn't just the fact that I had meet Sophie; it was what I had learnt from her. I knew more about being *pushed* than I had let on. Just like Isidor – I knew more. Just like the photograph had been left for Isidor, those letters – my love letters – had been sent to Sophie. Each one of them had been mysteriously pushed through her letterbox. Those letters of mine had ruined her relationship with her lover in this world. More than that, they had led her to me again. They had brought us back together, and I wondered now if Isidor's photograph hadn't brought him and Melody back together in some other *when*. One thing I did know for sure, just like the photograph which had been left for Isidor to find, the letters had ultimately led to Sophie's death. Just like the photograph had led to Isidor's death.

Now Kiera had a photograph of her and her father – the word *PUSH* scribbled across the back. Would that picture lead to her death just like it had for the others? Someone was seriously fucking with us all and I wondered if Murphy knew that. Is that why he had suddenly broken cover and come back? Still, I wish he had given me some warning. I didn't like being caught with my trousers down. I looked at him again, and although I was glad to see my friend, I was so pissed at him that before I knew what I was doing, I had whispered, "Thanks for the warning, *friend*."

"What are you talking about?" he whispered back from the corner of his mouth.

"Yeah, what are you talking about?" Kayla asked from the back of the van.

Suddenly remembering that there wasn't much she didn't hear, I glanced back at her. Kayla sat on one side of Kiera, and Sam on the other. All three were staring at me. I looked at Kiera and could see the distrust in her eyes for me. There was something more than that, though; she looked hurt.

"Potter's known for some time that Murphy, just like us, came back from the dead," Kiera breathed, not taking her eyes off me for one second.

"Why would you keep something like that from your friends?" Kayla gasped, throwing me an accusing stare.

I looked back at Murphy and hissed, "Any time you want to jump in and help out here will be fine with me."

"How much do they know?" he whispered from the corner of his mouth again. "Did you tell her about her father?"

"Yes," I nodded, feeling three sets of eyes boring into me from the shadows at the back of the van.

"Sophie?" he hushed.

"Who's Sophie?" Kayla piped up. "I've never heard of anyone called Sophie before."

"I have," Kiera whispered.

I cringed at the sound of the hurt in her voice. "Now why did you go and say something like that?" I barked at Murphy.

"Sorry," he glanced at me. "Shit, I thought perhaps you'd told her everything."

"No," I hissed.

"No?" he said, cocking an eyebrow at me.

"You told me not to!" I roared at him.

"I told you not to say anything about me or her dad," Murphy snapped back. "What you say and don't say about one of your ex-girlfriends is up to you."

"A girlfriend?" Sam smirked.

"Hey, listen up, wolf-boy this has nothing to do with you!" I snapped back at him.

"Sorry," he smirked back, enjoying my obvious discomfort.

"I think I preferred you in the coma," I said.

"It's a shame the same can't be said about you," Kiera remarked, springing out of her seat. "Stop the van, Murphy. I'm getting out!"

Chapter Seven

Kiera

"I said stop the van!" I yelled, screwing my hands into fists at my sides.

The police van lurched to the side as Murphy steered it off road and into a nearby field. He applied the brakes, coming to a juddering halt. Just wanting to be away from Potter – wanting to be on my own – I kicked open the back doors and leapt into the grass. The ground felt mushy beneath my boots from the heavy rainfall of the last twenty-four hours. It was cold and I wrapped my coat about me, heading away from the van and across the bleak-looking field.

"Hey, Kiera!" Potter called after me.

Before I'd had the chance to tell him to go screw himself, he was beside me and grabbing my arm.

"Let go of me!" I shouted, tugging my arm free. His grip was tight and he held me firm.

"Listen to me, tiger!" he said, trying to keep his voice calm – steady. "It's not what you think."

"Don't you dare call me that!" I shouted, just inches from his face. "I'm not your tiger – sweet-cheeks – or anything else. Why don't you just fuck off?"

"I know I've been keeping secrets from you, but I've had my reasons," Potter tried to explain.

"He's right," Murphy called climbing from the van and landing in the mud. His feet made a squelching sound. He looked down at his slippers which were now covered in mud. "Oh sweet Jesus," he groaned.

"Is that all you're worried about?" I snapped at him as he stood looking down at his feet in the pale morning light.

"I've had these for years," he grumbled at me.

Looking in disbelief at both Murphy and Potter, I said, "You two really are just a couple of freaking jokers. You two just don't give a shit about anyone other than yourselves."

"Not true," Potter cut in.

"No?" I hissed. "So why didn't you tell me about the secrets the pair of you have been keeping?"

"To protect you," Potter said.

"Bullshit!"

"Potter is telling you the truth," Murphy said, slipping and sliding in the mud as he came towards me.

"So keeping secrets about Sophie is protecting me, right?" I snapped, tiny plumes of breath escaping from my mouth and disappearing upwards.

Murphy glanced at Potter, and lighting his pipe, he said, "Yeah, what was it with the whole Sophie thing?"

"Look, will you stop keep going on about fucking Sophie!" Potter barked at him. "Can't you see you've dropped me in enough shit already?"

"I didn't tell you to go and see Sophie," Murphy snapped back, shoving his pipe into the corner of his mouth. "That was your bright idea, not mine."

"But you were the one who told me not to tell Kiera I had seen you and that her father was still alive!" Potter said, desperate to shove some of the blame back in Murphy's direction.

Staring at them opened-mouthed as they bickered like a couple of schoolboys before me, I said, "I don't care whose idea it was. Neither of you should have lied to me. I thought we were friends."

"We are friends," Murphy came back at me.

I looked at him and could see that he didn't have the faintest idea how their secrets had made me feel. "Do you know how it felt to watch you – my so-called friend – get ripped to pieces beneath the Fountain of Souls? Do you?"

Murphy stared back at me, his eyes crystal blue, and pipe smoke curling up from the end of his pipe.

"It broke my fucking heart!" I yelled at him. "You became more than just a friend to me, you became like a father. I wanted you to be like a father to me, because I had to sit and watch mine be eaten away by cancer, until he was nothing more than a bunch of bones screaming out in pain like a wild animal. Then when I had to stand and watch you get your heart ripped out, then set upon by those wolves, I realised I knew how it must have felt to have your heart ripped out, because that's how I felt when I saw my own father screeching in agony, as he begged the nurses for more morphine to take away the pain. I never thought I would feel like that again – but thanks to you two arseholes, I feel that pain again. You've both known that my father is still alive, and yet neither of you could tell me."

"He's not your father," Murphy said, his voice now soft, his usual gruff tone gone, like the plumes of breath which disappeared above me.

"Potter said he had seen him!" I snapped.

"I saw someone who looks like your father, Kiera," he said. "But he isn't the father you describe, screaming out in pain with cancer."

"Well that's good, isn't it?" I shot back at him. "At least there is some redeeming feature in this world which has been *pushed.*"

"But he isn't the man you remember," Murphy said. "He doesn't know you. He knows another Kiera. That's the Kiera he loves. The Kiera he fetched up as his own."

"There are two of me here?" I breathed, feeling as if my head had just been plunged into a bucket of ice-cold water.

"The Kiera from this world is dead," Murphy explained. "Just like you, she was a cop, but she got shot dead in the line of duty."

"What about my mother?" I gasped, wondering if in this *pushed* world, she was a Vampyrus.

"She died giving birth to you," Murphy said. "So as you can see, there are similarities between the world – the when – we knew, and this one. Both here and there your mother is dead, and so are you, Kiera."

"But things aren't the same," I breathed, my mind working overtime as I tried to make sense of what I was being told.

"What do you mean?" Potter asked me.

"My father is still very much alive here," I said, staring straight at him. "And I want to see him."

"And that's why we didn't tell you," Murphy said, taking the pipe from his mouth. "I knew you would want to see him, it would only be natural. But you can't."

"Why not?" I snapped. "I have a right to, he's my father."

"You have no rights here, Kiera," Murphy said. "You shouldn't be here."

"Says who?"

"The Kiera from this *when* is dead," Potter said. "She's buried in a cemetery. *Her* father visits the grave each morning on his way to work."

"But I'm not dead," I insisted. "Maybe that's why I'm here – to be reunited with my father again."

"That's not the reason why you are here," Potter said, taking my arm again. "We're here because someone is jerking us off. They're yanking our chain – taking the piss – messing with our heads. Whatever way you look at it, someone is seriously fucking with us and we need to find out who."

"How can you be so sure?" I asked, my eyes narrowing as I stared at him. What else hadn't he told me?

"Because of what happened when I found Sophie again," Potter said, looking away.

"So what did happen?" I said, unable to hide the resentment and bitterness in my voice. "Why did you go and look her up? I thought you told me she broke your heart once?"

"She did," Potter said, still unable to look at me.

"So why go in search of her?" I sneered. "Wanted one last fling?"

"No," Potter said, now turning to face me. "I needed to know what was going on in this new world we had been brought back to. Other than you, I knew no one here. Murphy was dead – or so I thought at the time. I didn't know anyone else other than Sophie. So when I left Hallowed Manor that day, I went in search of her. I met her father and he spoke of Skin-walkers who had come looking for her. There were other things, too, which were different. She hadn't studied music like she had in the world we had come from. So I decided not to pursue her and I went to your flat. It was my intention to get some of your belongings and come straight back to the manor and you."

"So what kept you?" I asked, the sound of suspicion in my voice barely hidden. "You were gone more than twenty-four hours. Enough time to pick me out some clean clothes."

"I broke into your flat but I wasn't the only one there," Potter explained, taking a cigarette and lighting it. "Sophie had got there before me."

"What was *she* doing in my flat?" I demanded, unable to bear the thought of the both of them together, especially there. That was my private place – that was my home.

"She was looking for you, Kiera," he said, thin jets of blue smoke pouring from his nostrils.

"Looking for me?" I frowned. "Why?"

"Because you sat bolt upright on her mortuary slab and fled the hospital," he said, looking straight at me.

"What?" I gasped, my brain feeling as if it had been wrung dry like a dirty dishcloth.

"Like I've tried to explain," Potter said. "Things in this world aren't the same and I'm not just talking about a few rock bands and story books. Sophie wasn't a musician in this *when*, she was a pathologist and you found your way onto her mortuary slab. Now what are the chances of that happening, I wonder?"

"But why?" I gasped, unable to think of anything else to say.

"I know it's a bit of a mind-fuck," Potter breathed out smoke. "But that's what I've been trying to tell you."

I was quiet for a moment, as I tried to comprehend everything I had been told. Then looking straight at Potter, I said, "Did she remember you? Did she remember what you had once shared together?"

"Eventually," Potter said, flicking the butt of his cigarette away.

"What's that s'posed to mean?"

"When we were chained together in the caves beneath the Fountain of Souls, do you remember me telling you that I once wrote letters to Sophie? He asked me.

"Yes," I said, nodding my head. "You told me they were love letters."

"Even though my letters were written before the world had been *pushed*," Potter started, "they found their way into this *when*. Someone managed to get hold of those letters and deliver them to her – as if trying to evoke old memories in her. Eventually they did, and she remembered me."

"Where is she now?" I asked him.

"I don't know," Potter said. "I took her to this farmhouse where she had been hiding from the Skin-walkers who were searching for her. But they tracked us there. She ran out into the road in fear and was run down by a car." Then looking away in shame, he whispered, "I left her there on the road."

"So why were the Skin-walkers hunting her?" I asked.

"Because of you," Murphy said.

I looked at him. "Because of me?"

"She snuck a vial of your blood from the mortuary," Murphy explained. "Sophie knew you were different – I mean, what sort of human wakes up on the slab and heads straight for the door? But word got back to the Skin-walkers about what had happened to you."

"Why was I so important to them?"

"For hundreds of years the Skin-walkers have been waiting for an angel to come," Murphy said, staring at me. "They knew that she would be dead. She would have wings like a dead angel and be made of dead flesh. They believe that she would come and destroy the treaty between man and wolf. They fear that her coming will bring the end to the wolves."

"And they believe that I am this messiah – this dead angel who will destroy the wolves?" I asked him.

"You are the dead angel the wolves fear," Murphy said.

"But who knew that I would come?" I quizzed him. "Who told the wolves of this prophecy?"

"The one who calls himself the wolfman," Murphy said.

"Who is this wolfman?" I pushed, wondering once again if he were keeping more secrets from me.

"I don't know," Murphy said. "I've been trying to find out. That's why I asked Potter not to mention my return. The fewer people who knew, the better chance I had of working undetected by the wolves."

"So you don't trust me then?" I asked. "Do you really think I would betray you?"

"Not willingly," Murphy grunted. "But who knows what a wolf might seduce from you. A wolf like Jack Seth."

"Do you think he is this wolfman?" I asked him.

"No," Murphy said with a shake of his head.

"How can you be so sure?" Now it was Potter's turn to question his friend.

"Seth is being punished by the Elders just like the rest of us," Murphy said. "He hasn't the brains to put something like this in place. No, there is someone more powerful than Seth with all the strands in their hands."

"He tucked us up good and proper over the death of McCain," Potter said. "He deceived us all because Kiera failed to choose between the humans and the Vampyrus in The Hollows. He's been working with this wolf called Elizabeth Clarke and an Oompa Loompa named Dorsey."

"Never heard of no wolf by that name," Murphy said thoughtfully. Then looking at Potter again, he said, "What the fuck is an Oompa Loompa?"

"It doesn't matter," I cut in with a shake of my head. I wasn't in the mood to stand and listen to Potter talk about the cast of *Willy Wonka and the Chocolate Factory*.

"Let's just say Seth has a pretty big grudge against Kiera and let's be honest, he isn't too tightly wrapped. It's because of him and the trap he set back at Ravenwood School that the Treaty of Wasp Water has collapsed, and the Skin-walkers are taking over."

"Seth is just a fly in the ointment," Murphy tried to assure us. "There is someone far more dangerous than him."

"This wolfman?" I asked him.

"Yes – whoever that might be," Murphy said. "I've tried to get close to him, but every line of investigation leads to just a small link in a far longer chain. A chain which will lead us to him – but a chain that seems to have no end. Someone is playing a very dark game with us. It's like we're on a chess board. Just like statues which are being moved around in some sick game."

I was quiet for a moment as the wind grew steadily stronger around us. Kayla and Sam sat in the back of the van, watching us.

"What about Isidor?" I asked Potter.

"What about him?"

"That photograph found its way to him, just like the letters you sent found their way back to Sophie," I reminded him. "Isidor is dead now and so is Sophie. Whoever sent that picture and those letters did it because they knew that Isidor and Melody had once loved each other, just like you and Sophie had."

"So?" Potter said.

"You just don't see it, do you?" I said, slapping my forehead with the heel of my hand.

"See what?"

"Whoever is behind all of this is targeting people we loved," I told him. "They are slowly killing them off one by one. The picture of my father, with the word *push* on the back was a warning."

"What picture?" Murphy cut in.

"Potter brought a picture of me and my father back from my flat, and just like on the back of Isidor's picture, someone had written the word *push*. It's a warning," I said, my stomach starting to knot in dread.

"What kind of warning?" Potter snapped.

"That my father is going to be killed next," I breathed.

"How many ways have I got to explain this – that man isn't your father," Potter said, his voice brimming with despair.

"Maybe, maybe not," I said thoughtfully. "But he still doesn't deserve to die because I failed to make a choice. I can't just sit back quietly knowing that someone is about to die because of me."

Taking me by the shoulders, Potter stared at me and said, "Who says that it's your father who is going to die? It could be you, Kiera. The trap could've been set for you."

"That may be so, but none of us can be sure of that," I said. I couldn't go on knowing that my father was going to die another hideous death – but this time because of me. How would I be able to live with that? Then, looking at Murphy, I said, "Where does my father live in this world?"

"Kiera, forget it," Murphy barked at me.

"I can't," I whispered with tears welling in the corners of my eyes. "I've got to go and save him. I couldn't last time, but this time around I have a chance of putting something right. If that's all I do in this world which has been *pushed* – then my coming back has some meaning."

"But you can't save him any more than I could save Sophie, or save Isidor," Potter tried to warn me. "If that car hadn't had hit Sophie, then the wolves would have got her in the end and..."

"...And just like we couldn't persuade Isidor to leave the station with us," I cut in, "you can't convince me not to go and try and save my father." Then looking at Murphy, I added, "Now give me my father's address."

"He's not your father," Murphy whispered, his eyes looking wet.

"He's the nearest thing that I've got to one," I said, guessing I would hurt Murphy by those words. I still felt hurt by him and Potter. Angry.

"Don't tell her," Potter snapped at Murphy.

"Fine," I said. "I'll find him myself. I'm sure I can read a phonebook."

Then as I turned my back on the both of them, I heard Murphy reluctantly whisper the address. I looked back at him.

"Thank you," I whispered.

"I don't believe you?" Potter hissed at Murphy. "What did you go and tell her for?"

"We can't stop her from going," Murphy snapped back.

"But I thought you said it was a stupid fucking idea to go and look for him," Potter said.

"It is but..."

Before Murphy had a chance to finish, Potter looked at me and said, "I'm coming with you."

"No," I said. "This is something I have to do on my own."

"Why?"

"Why didn't you take me with you when you went in search of Sophie?" I asked him.

"That was different," he came back at me.

"Sure it's different. I haven't screwed the person I'm going back to save," I said, turning away. Then stopping and looking back at him I added, "Did you?"

"Did I do what?" he asked, his eyes growing dark.

"Sleep with her – when you found each other again?" I whispered, tears spilling onto my cheeks and hating them. I didn't want Potter to see me cry. He didn't deserve to see my hurt. He had no right.

"What do you think?" he asked back.

"I guess it doesn't matter what I think," I said, looking at him. "Or you would've never gone looking for her again."

Then, turning my back on him and the others, I set off across the field.

"Kiera," I heard Murphy call after me. "There is a house on the other side of this hill. We'll wait until this time tomorrow morning, then we'll have to move on again. It's too dangerous for us to stay in the same place for too long."

Without looking back, I brushed the tears from my cheeks and went in search of my father.

Chapter Eight

Potter

"Well done!" Murphy said, turning back towards the police van.

"What's that s'posed to mean?" I asked, the wind picking up and making the long grass bend to and fro.

"You've gone and upset Kiera now," he said, lifting his leg and trying to shake the mud from his slipper.

"It wasn't my fucking idea to go and lie to her," I snapped in resentment. "That was yours."

"I meant looking up your old girlfriend!" Then turning to face me, he said, "Potter, at what point did you think that was a good idea?"

"I was desperate," I said, remembering how lost I had felt in those first few weeks after returning from The Hollows. "You were dead – or so I thought. I needed to find out what was happening. I had no one else to turn to."

"Yeah, you did," Murphy grunted, giving up on his slippers which were now caked with mud. "You had Kiera. Why you feel the need to fool around when you have such a beautiful girl like Kiera in tow beats the shit out of me."

"I haven't been fooling around with anyone," I barked.

"Don't give me that crap," he said, his clear blue eyes fixing on mine. "You were upstairs in the bedroom with that Sophie getting your pecker wet when I showed up."

"Hey, listen!" I yelled, grabbing his arm, so he couldn't walk away. "I didn't have sex with Sophie, not in this world. I wouldn't do that to Kiera – I couldn't even if I'd wanted to, and the thing is – I didn't want to. I'm in love with Kiera – no one else."

56

"Well it's a shame you didn't tell her that," Murphy said, shrugging my hand free. "Perhaps she would've stayed."

"Kiera hasn't gone because of anything I've said or done," I told him. "She went because of her father."

"Jesus, Potter," Murphy groaned. "I worry about you sometimes. She left because of you and that tart, Sophie."

"Sophie wasn't a tart," I cut in.

"You're very defensive about someone you couldn't give two shits about," Murphy eyed me.

"Look, I'm not taking the blame!" I shouted. "This is your fuck-up as much as mine."

"How do you figure that?" Murphy frowned.

"You were the bright spark who thought it would be a good idea to keep all of this shit from Kiera, not me," I reminded him. "It was you who said not to tell her you were back. You didn't even break the news that you were back gently. Oh no, you had to turn up in a big white police van, with sirens screaming and lights flashing and shouting out about the Muppets. Fuck knows what the Muppets have to do with any of this!"

"It was *you* I was calling the Muppet!" Murphy roared, and prodded me twice in the chest with his forefinger.

"I ain't no Muppet!" I shot back, my chest feeling numb from where he had jabbed at me.

"Oh no?" Murphy hissed. "You could've fooled me. You went screaming across the roof of that train like fucking Beaker. All you needed was the bright orange hair and I would've never known the difference."

"If you hadn't noticed, we were being chased down by a pack of berserkers who wanted to tear our freaking heads off!" I roared back. "What else was I s'posed to do?"

"You're not meant to be drawing any unwanted attention to yourself, and here you are, running around like The

57

Terminator on crack," Murphy said. "And another thing! Who's the wolf? I thought you hated wolves!"

"I do," I snapped back. "Letting him tag along wasn't my bright idea. It was Kiera's. I think Kayla's gone and got herself all loved up!"

"What's he like?" Murphy asked.

"Who?"

"The Wolf!" Murphy growled. "Who else did you think I was talking about numb-nuts?"

"I wouldn't trust him," I said.

"Why not?" Murphy asked, cocking an eyebrow at me.

"Because he's a freaking wolf! Why else?"

"We'll see," murphy said thoughtfully and walked away.

As we neared the van, I could see Kayla and the wolf-boy sitting next to each other by the open doors, their legs dangling out of the back. Both of them were watching us as we approached. Kayla looked pale, her sprinkling of pink coloured freckles standing out like a rash in the cold.

Looking at the boy, Murphy said, "We haven't been introduced. My name is..."

"Kayla has just been telling me all about you," Sam cut in, his voice like a soft growl. "She told me you were once eaten by wolves."

"That's right," Murphy said eyeing him. "It's a good job for you I don't keep a grudge." Then Murphy was gone, climbing back into the van behind the driver's wheel.

"But I do," I said, looking at Sam, knowing that most of the troubles in my life had a wolf hidden not too far behind them. I left them sitting at the back of the van. As I reached the passenger door, Kayla called out to me.

"Potter, is Kiera coming back?"

Without looking back at her, I said, "I hope so, I really do." I climbed into the cab of the van, and swung the door shut.

Chapter Nine

Kiera

With my coat wrapped about me, and my hands thrust into the pockets, I made my way across the field, leaving Potter and the others behind me. Murphy had given me twenty-four hours to see my father and get back. I would take as long as I needed – who was he to make up the rules? How could they both have kept such secrets from me? Who did they think they were? At twenty years old, I didn't need them deciding what I should or shouldn't know. I had a right to know that my father was alive here – even if Murphy said I had no rights in this *pushed* world. I just wanted to see my father again, to know that he was all right, to know that he was alive. The need to push those last memories of him crying out for pain relief would be pushed aside, buried, if I could only see him again, looking well – alive. That's all I wanted to do; just to see him again.

Who wouldn't want to do that if they were given another chance? How many wouldn't want to go back and be able to say all the stuff they wished they had said to their loved one before it had been too late – before they had been taken from them? I was no different from anyone else, other than I had been given a second chance – an opportunity to see my father again. If I didn't, it would haunt me whether I stayed in this *pushed* world or not. I would spend my time here like a restless spirit. How could I rest knowing that my father was out there somewhere, within reach of me? It would drive me mental. It would drive me insane quicker than the need for blood does when it comes. It would be like that itch deep inside of me, which eventually turns into a craving, a hunger that can't be quenched until blood is washing over my tongue and cooling my throat. I had to see my father again – despite Murphy's and Potter's warnings.

Who was Potter to give me advice anyhow? I wondered, climbing over a wooden fence which circled the field. He hadn't wasted any time in going in search of Sophie. Why had he done that? Because he was still in love with her, right? I didn't care what he said, what excuses he made. The fact he went looking for her, before anyone else, said that he still had feelings for her, and I guessed he always would. Sophie was Potter's first true love, and did we ever forget them? I couldn't be sure – Potter was mine. Would I be able to shirk off the feelings that I had for him so easily? Probably not. Even though he was a complete cock at times – I knew there would always be a small part of me that felt something for him. That's what I hated, though. He had hurt me, deceived me; and although my feelings towards him were ones of distrust and hatred, I knew that deep inside of me I was still very much in love with him. It was hard to admit that, as it hurt to do so.

On the other side of the fence, I stumbled across a narrow path cut into the grass. It spiralled downwards and away to a small crop of trees. I looked back, and the police van and the others had gone. Feeling alone now, I faced front and headed towards the trees. With the wind tugging at my long hair, I bent forward into the wind.

Had he slept with Sophie again? I wondered. What did she look like? Potter had told me deep below the Fountain of Souls, as we lay chained together, that she had been beautiful. He told me about those letters, the ones in which he had pleaded for her to come back to him. I should have seen the signs back then. For someone who saw too many things sometimes – I had been blinded by him back in those caves. That had been the first time we had made love, our hands manacled together. Had we made love though? I thought we had, but did Potter feel the same? As he had sex with me, was he thinking about me or her – Sophie?

I headed towards the trees, feeling sick with jealousy and hurt. I felt stupid and used. How could I have been so naive? If Sophie had been in those caves with him instead of me, it would have been her he would have made love to. It would have been an act of love – not out of fear and desperation at the thought of dying. That one final act bringing us together before we died – or so we believed back then.

I tried to push the thoughts of paranoia from my mind, but as I neared the trees, those voices of doubt just wouldn't keep quiet. I tried to tell myself that Potter did love me, that there had been other times when we had been together – made love and it had been intense – it had been real. I tried to conjure all the times Potter told me how much he loved me while making love. There was the time in the summerhouse just before leaving Hallowed Manor. We had made love on the floor, and over and over again, he had told me how much he loved me. He had let me drink his blood, and he had drunk mine too. Then stopping up short, my skin turned cold and my stomach lurched.

"Oh, my God," I breathed aloud.

Moments before making love on the floor of the summerhouse, Potter had returned from her – from being with Sophie. He had led me away from the statue I had been looking at in the rain. Potter had taken me into the summerhouse, and as he had peeled my wet clothes from me and laid me down on the floor, he had been thinking of her. All the time he must have been thinking of Sophie. Potter had come straight back and tried to bury his own guilt and shame by having sex with me. I screwed my eyes shut as those images of us together taunted me.

I could remember Potter had been unusually gentle, covering my face, neck, shoulders, breasts, and stomach with soft kisses. I could hear the sound of the rain drumming against the summerhouse roof, and the gentle rise and fall of our breathing.

"I love you, Kiera," he had whispered against my cheek as he lowered himself onto me.

"I love you, too," I smiled, running my hands through his untidy hair. Then those images changed, and it wasn't me I could see beneath him, it was Sophie, and I was nothing more than the statue outside in the rain, peering in through the window.

With my stomach cramping, and feeling sick at the images of them together, I leant forward and gagged. A thin stream of vomit swung from my chin, and tears rolled down the length of my face. I armed the vomit away and sucked in two large mouthfuls of air. I staggered off from the path which entered the crop of trees. With my legs feeling like jelly beneath me, I fell against a tree and slid down the length of its trunk. I pulled my knees up against my chest, and covering my face with my hands, I cried. How could Potter hurt me like this? What had I done to deserve it?

I rocked backwards and forwards slowly beneath the canopy of trees and I couldn't care if I never saw Potter again. There was only one man that I wanted to be held and comforted by right now, and that was my father. Wiping snot from my upper lip and the tears from my cheeks, I stood up. I wouldn't waste another tear on Potter – he didn't deserve one of them. With the trees offering me a place to hide, I loosened my coat and released my wings. I trampled slowly over the mush of fallen leaves until I found a hole in the branches above me. The morning sky looked white, like a bed of snow. Spreading my wings, I tilted my head back, pressed my arms flat against my sides, and shot up into the sky, hiding myself and the pain amongst the clouds.

Chapter Ten

Potter

Murphy drove the police van to the rear of a rundown-looking cottage. The outside was weather-beaten white, but most of this was hidden by blotches of yellowy-green moss and ivy. The roof slated downwards and was covered in thick rows of grey slate. There was a chimney which leant to one side and looked as if it might just collapse into a pile of brick and dust at any moment.

"It's nice to see that you've kept up your high standards of living," I said, peering through the mud-splashed windscreen.

"The rent's cheap and it's remote," Murphy said, steering the van into an equally rundown-looking ramshackle of a barn. He killed the engine and climbed out, a trail of pipe smoke drifting out behind him. Once out of the police van, I followed Murphy, Kayla, and Sam out of the barn. Murphy swung the heavy-looking doors closed and headed towards the cottage. He took a key from his trouser pocket and opened the back door.

The kitchen was poky, but snug-looking. There was a cooker and stove, a sink, and a small, round table with chairs. Tatty-looking curtains hung over grimy windows, and Murphy pulled them shut, even though it was still morning. The kitchen was thrown into semi darkness. There was a lamp on the table and Murphy switched it on, but it did little to lighten the gloom. Murphy kicked off his mud-stained slippers and stood before us in a pair of threadbare socks. The big toe of his right foot stuck out through a hole in them. He left the kitchen and we followed him into a small living room. There was a dusty-looking two-seater sofa and a couple of mismatched armchairs. A staircase on my right disappeared up into darkness. Part of the stone floor was covered with a faded rug. Murphy knelt down before a stone fireplace set into the wall. The grate was piled with logs. We watched as he took some sheets of newspaper from a pile next to the fireplace. He rolled them up, twisting their ends into points. Then, taking his lighter from his shirt pocket, he lit the pieces of newspaper, and then stuffed them between the gaps in the logs.

"Make yourself comfortable," he said, once the logs started to smoulder.

Plumes of thick, grey smoke started to billow up the chimney and the room began to warm. Kayla and Sam sat next to one another on the sofa, a cloud of dust flying up from the cushions. Kayla placed a hand over her mouth and coughed. I sat in one of the armchairs.

"Soup anyone?" Murphy asked, looking at us, brushing soot from his hands.

"That would be great," Kayla said with a half-smile. By looking at her face, I guessed like me, she saw little point in eating anything other than the red stuff. Food had lost its taste since coming back from the dead.

"I'll have some," Sam said.

Murphy looked at me and I shook my head.

"Suit yourself," he grunted and went to the kitchen.

There was the sound of pots and pans clattering together. We sat in silence, watching the growing flames, until Murphy returned a short time later. He carried a pot by its handle and three mugs. Murphy hung the pot over the fire and placed the mugs on the small table next to his chair.

"This is all very cosy," I said, "but what next? We just sit and wait?"

"I said I would give Kiera twenty-four hours and I'm keeping my word," Murphy said, the soup now bubbling away over the fire.

The smell of it made my stomach lurch, but I just couldn't bring myself to eat anything. "What if she doesn't come back by this time tomorrow morning?"

"I don't know," Murphy shrugged. "We need to keep moving."

"We go and look for her, that's what we do," I said.

"She might not want you to," Kayla said, looking at me.

"You heard everything, didn't you?" I asked her. I could tell she was pissed at me.

"Of course," she said. "How could you lie to Kiera? I thought you two were, you know, in love?"

"Kayla, do me a favour and mind your own business," I said, looking away into the fire.

"It is my business," Kayla came straight back at me. "Kiera is like a sister to me. I've already lost my brother thanks to you."

Unable to believe what I was hearing, I looked back at her and said, "What the hell are you talking about?"

"You killed Isidor," she said, staring back at me, her face a white mask of frustration and anger. "If you hadn't had always been at him – making him look stupid and calling him names – he would have come with us. He wouldn't have wanted to stay at that railway station."

"Listen, he didn't stay because of anything I did or said," I snapped at her. "He stayed because he was all loved-up with some tattooed tart."

"See, that's just what I'm talking about!" Kayla hissed, jumping up from the sofa. "You just can't stop being cruel to people. You think it's funny, but it's not. What you say hurts people. Just like you hurt Isidor, and now you've gone and hurt Kiera. How many more people are you going to drive away?"

"You don't know what you're talking about," I barked back at her.

"What makes you so special that you can go around taking the piss out of people?" she snapped back at me, her face livid and drawn-looking. Suddenly she did look older than her sixteen years. "You're far from perfect, with your stinking tobacco breath, big nose, and smart mouth. Fuck knows what Kiera ever saw in you!"

"My ready wit and charm, I guess," I smirked at her.

"See, you never take anything seriously," Kayla snapped, and she looked close to tears. "Why can't you just stop being cruel to people? You used to really hurt Isidor with some of the stuff you said. You couldn't even remember his name half of the time. You were always calling him Shaggy-Doo and a whole load of other shit. Isidor might not have been as clever as you think you are, but he was a good person, a kind person, and you took advantage of that. It was because of you he stayed behind in that station – not because of Melody Rose. He was hurting and couldn't put up with you bullying him anymore, and now you've gone and driven Kiera away."

"You don't know what you're talking..." but before I'd had the chance to finish, Kayla had fled the room, racing up the stairs. The sound of a door slamming closed echoed from above.

I looked across the room at Murphy. He stared back at me from beneath his bushy white eyebrows, pipe jutting from the corner of his mouth. "Well done, Potter. You've gone and upset her now," he grunted at me.

Sam looked at me too, the fire reflecting back from within his bright yellow eyes.

"What?" I snapped at him.

"You did use to call Isidor Shaggy-Doo," he said softly. "And you've already called me Teen-Wolf and Captain Caveman twice."

"Ah, for fuck's sake! I can't believe what I'm hearing," I groaned, getting up from my chair. "I need some air."

Feeling like a piece of shit, I left the cottage and the sound of Kayla's fit of hysterics behind me.

Chapter Eleven

Kiera

The address Murphy had given me for my father's home wasn't the same place where I had grown up with him in my other life. He lived close by, but not the same. I guess that was only to be expected in a world which had been pushed. There were slight differences everywhere. The clouds were bitterly cold, and before long, my face had begun to turn numb. The clouds were heavy with moisture and I knew that as the wind grew colder, they would soon be shedding snow onto the world below.

As I raced back towards Havensfield, and the place near to where I grew up in the south west of England, my face, arms, and legs grew colder and colder until it was difficult for me to feel them at all. I dropped through the clouds, just low enough to see the lay of the ground below, to get my bearings and try to figure out how far I was from home. Home? That seemed a strange kind of word to use. It wasn't my home – not the place where I had been raised. I wondered who now lived in that house I had shared with my father, snuggled up on his lap as he read books like the Brothers Grimm to me. I wonder who slept in my old bedroom. Was there another little girl living there, fearing that one day the wolves would come demanding to be matched with her? How would her parents let her go? Give her up? They had to, right? That was the law in this new world, where an uneasy peace had been found between the humans and the Skin-walkers. Hadn't that treaty been dissolved now because of the trickery Jack Seth had played with me? The death of McCain had seen to that.

With Truro racing past below, I knew I was about five miles away from where my father now lived. If I remembered rightly, it was a hamlet just on the outskirts of Havensfield. I didn't know it well, but I would find it. Being so close to seeing my father again, I began to feel nervous. What would he say when he saw me? Would he be pleased?

You're not his, Kiera, Murphy's warning rang in my ears. *His Kiera is dead.*

I tried to push his voice away, let it mingle with the sound of the roaring wind that rushed all around me. However, it just wouldn't go. Murphy's voice wasn't just in the wind. It was inside my head, too. As I flew ever closer, I knew deep down inside of me that Murphy was right. What would my father think if I suddenly appeared at his front door? He'd think I was a ghost come back from the dead. I couldn't stay with him forever. I'd have to leave again, and that would break his heart twice over. Could I really do that to him? No, I couldn't.

Even though Murphy's reasoning was clearing my thoughts and mind, that hunger to see my father again was just as strong. Like the need for blood, it just wouldn't go away unless sated somehow. The only way I would ever rid myself of that feeling was to see my father again. To see him from a distance, perhaps? Just another picture of him to cherish other than the one I had of him begging for pain relief.

With that numb feeling now spreading up my arms and legs and across my body, I brought my hands up in front of my face and gasped. My fingers and the palms of my hands were covered in tiny little cracks. How long had it been since I had last drank any blood? It had been in the bathroom at the station, when I had drunk some of Potter's. Without the red stuff, I knew my body would start to crack, turn grey, just like a statue. In my haste to get away from Potter and go in search of my father, I had forgotten to take any of the Lot 13 that Kayla carried with her in her rucksack. I'd been getting by on the blood I sucked from Potter. I had been reluctant to get hooked on Lot 13, but without either, I would surely end up like one of those statues in the grounds of Hallowed Manor.

Realising that it wasn't the cold which was making my body feel numb, I looked sideways at my wings. Just like my flesh, cracks had started to appear in them. Even those little claws at the tip of each of my wings had started to change from black to a dark chalky-grey. As I raced through the clouds, my wings began to feel heavier and more difficult to beat up and down. Slowly I started to drop towards the ground, not because I wanted to, but because I was becoming too heavy to stay in the air.

I was still some way off from my father's house and I knew I needed somewhere secluded to land for fear of being seen. Below me, I could see a desolate-looking graveyard. The church spire stood high in the air, and I aimed as best as I could towards it. Swooping around in the air like a kite that was being dragged back towards the ground, I fell out of the sky. With my wings now feeling like two dead weights, I clattered into the church spire. The air was forced from my lungs and I cried out. The tips of my wings scraped against the rough stone of the church, throwing up a thick spray of brick dust. Below, I could see a row of ancient-looking gravestones rushing up towards me.

I bounced off one of them and screamed out in pain as my head made a sickening thudding sound against the ground. The spire seemed to spin around in the sky above me as I lay on my back, feeling dazed and bruised. The corners of my vision started to turn black, like an old TV set with a damaged tube. I tried to keep my eyes open. Slowly, I twisted my head to the right and found myself looking up into the cracked face of a statue. Then everything went black.

Chapter Twelve

Potter

With my back to the small cottage, I looked out across the fields in the direction Kiera had headed. I wanted to go after her. I knew now that I would never be able to talk her out of the idea of seeing her father, but I wanted to be with her when she did. Such a thing wouldn't be easy for Kiera, and I wanted to be there to support her when it happened. Would she want me there? No. She had made that crystal clear.

From behind me I could hear the sound of Kayla sobbing. I looked back over my shoulder and up at one of the bedroom windows where the sound of her crying came from. I had really fucked things up this time, but I couldn't go and take any of it back. I placed a cigarette in the corner of my mouth and looked back across the fields. Kayla's words seemed to float in the bitter wind that carried my cigarette smoke away. She had been right, I had taken the piss out of Isidor and I'd had no idea how much that had hurt him until the end. Didn't Kayla think that if I could take back what I'd said to him I would? I'd never meant anything by it. I'd just been jerking around, that was all.

Just like I could hear Kayla's angry voice, I could see Isidor standing alone in that waiting room, the picture of him and Melody in his hand. He had the same look in his eyes that Sophie had had as she held tightly to the letters which had been pushed through her letterbox. It was a look of hope. A look that Isidor might see Melody again, and a look that Sophie and I could be lovers again. Both were now dead, along with their hope. I thought of the last few minutes Isidor and I had spent in that waiting room. I tried to warn him about that photograph. I could hear myself talking to him.

"*Isidor, believe it or not, I know what it feels like to have a broken heart. I loved a girl once but she's gone now, and in a way, it was the best thing that could have happened to me, because I would've never met Kiera,*" I had told him.

"*But I haven't met anyone else, that's my point,*" Isidor tried to explain to me. "*I don't have anybody. Melody hasn't gone, she is here somewhere, we will meet again – the picture proves that.*"

To remember hearing him say that he had no one made me swallow hard. It had been difficult to hear it back then, but even more difficult for me to remember.

"*I know about pictures and stuff that seem to have been pushed between the two worlds, and no good will come of it,*" I had tried to warn him. "*But believe me, Isidor, that picture of you and Melody, just like the letters that got pushed over to the girl I once loved, only led to suffering, and eventually, her death. Please come with us, Isidor, I don't want to leave you behind.*"

Flicking my half-smoked cigarette away, I sniffed back the tears which were now leaking from the corners of my eyes as I remembered asking him to come with us. I really hadn't wanted to leave him behind.

"*I'm staying, Potter, I know what I'm doing,*" Isidor had said.

Then with tears rolling off my chin, I heard myself say to Isidor, "*I'm sorry. I never meant to put you down or hurt you. You are my friend – you're my brother.*"

I was sorrier than anyone would ever know. If I could go back, I would have dragged Isidor from that waiting room. I wouldn't have let him stay, even if I'd had to fight with him. Not because I was in the shit now, but because I missed him. He was my friend – he had been like a younger brother to me and I shouldn't have left him behind. Teasing him with a few names hadn't been my crime, leaving him behind had.

Then, just like I had in that waiting room, I whispered aloud, "I'm sorry, Isidor."

How was I ever going to put things right with Kayla again? With Kiera again? Both of them thought I was a dick and they were probably both right about that. With the wind drying my tears, I looked back up at the window. The sound of Kayla's sobs had stopped. Not wanting to go back into the house and face Murphy's and Sam's accusing stares, but needing to speak to Kayla, I opened my wings and flew the short distance up to her window. I hovered outside, cupping my hands against the glass, and peering inside. Kayla lay on a narrow bed in the far corner, her back to the window and me. Taking a deep breath, I tapped against the windowpane. Startled, she glanced back over her shoulder. Seeing it was me, she jabbed her middle finger in the air, and lay back down again.

Nice! She was feeling better already, I thought. That was the Kayla I knew and loved.

I tapped against the window again with my knuckles.

"Fuck off!" I heard her muffled reply from behind the glass.

I tapped again.

"I said, Fuck off, Potter!" she shouted louder than the first time.

I tapped against the window once more.

Then through the glass, I watched as she sat up, swung her legs over the side of the bed and came marching towards the window. Her hair was angry red, and her eyes were cold blue.

"What part of fuck off don't you understand?" she shouted, hands on her hips.

"Let me in, Kayla, its freezing out here," I said through the glass.

"Good!" she snapped. "I hope you freeze to death."

"Don't be like that," I said softly. "I just wanted to talk to you."

"I can hear you just fine from in here," she snapped back.

"I can't talk to you from out here," I said. "Go on, let me in. Just give me five minutes, and if you're still mad at me after that, I promise to fuck off and never come back."

With her eyes fixed on mine, and her face beginning to soften, she said, "Potter, have you been crying?"

"Yes," I said, knowing that if I were ever to win her trust I had to be honest. I'd had enough of lies and bullshit to last me a lifetime.

"How come?" she asked me.

"Because of what happened to Isidor," I said, my nose almost touching the windowpane now. "But not just that. I feel bad for hurting you and Kiera. I never meant to. I promise."

Slowly, Kayla reached out and opened the window. "You've got five minutes," she whispered and let me in.

Chapter Thirteen

Kiera

"Help me!" the voice called. It was little more than a whisper, but it was there all the same.

"Help me!" the voice came again. It was the sound of a child. Boy or girl, I couldn't be sure.

I opened my eyes to find myself standing before a sea of statues. They stretched out before me for as far as the eye could see. Some looked away from me, as if scared – or out of some kind of misplaced reverence. The statues were grey or white in colour. Some looked more weather-stained than others – as if they had been here longer than the rest. I looked back to get my bearings and could see the church behind me, its spire reaching up into the gunmetal grey sky. I was right, it was going to snow, and the first flakes swept lazily down from above. The graveyard was still – quiet. Not even the barren black branches of the nearby trees stirred in the breeze. I looked back at the statues and flinched backwards. All of them now were looking away from me. How had they moved? The statues either covered their eyes with their arms or their hands.

"Help me!" the voice came again.

I tilted my head to the side as I tried to pinpoint the location of the soft, childlike voice.

"Help me!" it whispered again.

I looked front and knew that the voice was coming deep from within the maze of statues which had crammed themselves into the graveyard.

"Where are you?" I called out, my voice sounding thin and weak as it echoed back off the statues.

"Help me!" the voice came again.

I looked between the gaps the statues had made. There were so many of them, I wondered if I would barely be able to squeeze between them in search of the voice. Then I jumped. The sudden sound of the church bells ringing filled the air behind me. I looked back over my shoulder at the spire. One side of it was now covered white with snow. The bells stopped. With my mouth feeling dry, I looked back at the statues and gasped, a small cloud of breath escaping from my mouth. The statues had moved again. It was like they had stepped aside, making a path for me to walk between them. This time their faces were tilted skywards, flakes of snow settling over their blank eyes and faces. Their arms were out stretched and their fingers were entwined. All of them were holding hands. In a perverse way, they looked beautiful, tranquil, and I suddenly felt at peace.

"Help me!" the voice called again. But this time it added another word to that sentence and it made me shiver. "Please!"

Slowly putting one foot in front of the other, I stepped between the statues in search of the voice. I looked left and right at the statues. They weren't dressed in long, flowing gowns like so many statues you see in graveyards. They didn't look like angels either. They looked like everyday people who had somehow been turned to stone. There were children, some as young as four or five, teenagers, and adults. Men and women; boys and girls. Some of the women wore dresses, others denims, blouses, and coats. The men wore trousers, boots, and hats. Their style of clothing seemed to span several different time periods.

The snow fell heavier now, and I looked back to see how far I had come. I could no longer see the gap that the statues had seemed to open for me. It was as if they had gathered around the opening, their hands locked together preventing my exit. I could see my footprints in the snow, trailing away into the distance. I looked up and could see the church, faint in the distance, its spire white against the sky.

"Help me! Pleeeaaassee!" the voice hushed, this time closer now. As I drew nearer to the voice, it lost that childlike quality and sounded more like that of a young woman.

"Where are you?!" I called out.

Silence; not even the sound of the wind.

I looked back once more, my footprints now covered by the falling snow. Looking front again, I shivered; not with the cold, but through fear. The statues had changed position again. This time they were looking at me. A hundred or more sets of eyes were boring into me. Their cracked faces didn't look mean or angry, though. They looked kind of sad.

"Who are you?" I asked one of them, a boy about the age of sixteen. He looked familiar somehow. It was like I had seen him before someplace, but just couldn't quite remember where. He didn't answer me, he just stared, his snow-white eyes looking into mine. Slowly, I cupped one of my hands and pressed it softly against his handsome face then pulled it quickly away again. He didn't feel cold like stone, but warm, like a living person.

"Why are you here?" I asked, my mind thinking back to the statue of the girl in the grounds of Hallowed Manor. "Can I help you?"

The statue just stared back at me, its surface cracked and broken, his face covered with blotches of moss. I stepped away and followed the path the statues had created for me.

"Help me," the voice came again, this time more desperate sounding than before.

I quickened my step and rounded a bend in the path. Between the falling flakes of snow, I could see a clearing amongst the statues and I headed towards it. Standing at the edge of the clearing I could see it was circular in shape, and the statues surrounded it, all of their hands locked together like some weird child's game of 'a ring of roses.' In the centre of the clearing stood a statue. Its back was towards me, head cast down, arms outstretched on either side of it, palms facing upwards. Snow had gathered in the statue's hands, and it looked as if it were holding a fistful of soft, white feathers.

"Help me," the statue whispered. Although with its head facing away from me, and I couldn't see its lips move, I knew it had spoken.

With snow falling all around me, covering my hair and shoulders, I stepped into the clearing and towards the statue. My feet crunched in the snow, and if I'd had a heart, I knew it would have been racing.

Slowly I reached the statue and faced it. I could see by its long lengths of cracked and marble-looking hair, that it was female.

"I want to help you," I whispered, but the sound of my voice suddenly got drowned out by another sound – the sound of weeping. I looked left and right, and could see that the statues were no longer holding hands. Each had covered their faces and was crying into their hands. The sound of their weeping was like listening to a hundred lost children crying for their mothers. An unbearable sadness washed over me as I looked at them, young and old, all bent forward, weeping uncontrollably.

"Help me!" the voice suddenly whispered through the weeping.

I looked front to see that the statue had now raised its head and was looking back at me. Stumbling backwards, I threw my hands to my face and cried out. Looking at the statue was like looking at me. The statue *was* me. Although its face was cracked, and eyes a blank white, it was me I was looking at.

The statue spoke again, and instead of saying, "Help me," it whispered, "Help us!"

Its lips didn't move, not a fraction, but I could hear the voice all the same. It was like I could hear it in my head, and it was my own voice talking to me.

"Help us," my voice whispered inside my head again.

Trying to stay on my feet, I stared back at the statue of myself and whispered, "How do I help you?"

"Lead us to the Dead Waters," it breathed inside my head. "We will follow you."

"Who are you?" I asked, my voice barely audible over the sound of the sobbing coming from the statues that surrounded us.

"I am what you will become," the statue spoke again inside my mind, its dead, white eyes never leaving mine. "Don't let yourself become a statue, Kiera Hudson. Don't become one of us before you reach the Dead Waters."

"What are these Dead Waters?" I asked.

"Dead to the living, but not to us," the statue said.

"What does that mean?" I asked, my mind wondering if it wasn't some kind of a riddle.

"The dead waters will give us life, and you can't *push* back without us," the statue's voice hushed inside of me.

"How do I *push* back?" I whispered, the snow now so deep it covered my boots completely.

"Bathe in the Dead Waters if you want to save your friends," the statue said, and this time I detected a note of urgency in its voice – my voice inside of me.

"But my friends are safe, aren't they?" I asked, wiping away the snow that fell before my eyes. When I looked again, the statue was pointing behind me.

"What do you see, Kiera Hudson?" it asked me.

Slowly, I turned around, and this time my legs did buckle beneath me, and I fell to the ground, knee-deep in soft snow.

"Isidor?" I cried, ice-cold tears on my cheeks.

He stood before me, his arms wrapped around another – a girl – Melody Rose. The statue of Isidor and Melody stood locked in an eternal embrace, their dead, white eyes staring into each other's forever. Snow covered them. I crawled forward, my hands looking raw with the cold. There was another pair of statues just behind those of Isidor and Melody.

"Murphy," I cried out. He stood holding the hands of two beautiful-looking girls. I recognised one of the statues to be that of the girl I had seen in the grounds of Hallowed Manor holding the crucifix. My voice told me he was with his daughters, Meren and Nessa. He looked happy, snow gathering in his thick, white eyebrows and on the tops of his carpet slippers.

The snow whipped all around me, and I cupped my hands around my eyes. Two other statues appeared out of the snow. "Kayla?" I whispered. It was her, a block of cracked stone as she held Sam in her arms. He didn't look like a wolf though. He looked like the boy Isidor had carried from the burning school grounds. Frozen smiles tugged at the corners of their mouths. I looked back at the statue of me, but I had gone, replaced by another. Potter stood where the statue of me had once been. Dragging myself, I stumbled through the blizzard like snow towards it. I was there after all. Potter was holding me in his arms; my head was pressed gently against his chest.

"Potter," I breathed, waving the snow away from in front of my eyes. It was then I felt as if my very soul had been crushed inside of me. It wasn't me Potter was cradling in his arms, but another. She was beautiful – so beautiful. Sobbing into my hands, just like the hundreds of statues surrounding me, I knew it was Sophie he was holding.

"Potter," I sobbed, my soul aching. "Why?"

"Don't they all look happy?" the voice spoke up inside of me once more. This time the voice sounded different though. Old and broken.

I took my hands from my face and looked up into the falling snow. The statue of Potter and Sophie had gone. In their place stood statues of the four Elders. Beneath their stone hoods I could see their stitched-together faces, hard like marble.

"Don't your friends look happy?" one of them spoke. I couldn't tell which, as their cracked and blistered lips didn't move.

"Yes," I sobbed, unable to bear the memory of Potter and Sophie together.

"Don't you want your friends to finally find peace and happiness?" one of them asked, its voice almost teasing.

"Yes," I murmured, still on my knees.

"Then *push* everything back," another of them said. "*Push* back into place what you moved."

"I didn't move anything," I sobbed into the balls of my hands.

"Oh, Kiera," one of them said, as if they almost cared. "You failed to choose in The Hollows, and this is the result. Can't you *see* what you've done?"

"Everything would have been so simple if only you had chosen between the humans and the Vampyrus," explained another. "There can only be one. This *pushed* world is the result of you failing to make your choice."

"But I couldn't choose," I shouted at them, driving my fists into the snow. "You asked the impossible! You choose!"

"And that is why we are here. That is why we look the way we do," and all of them seemed to speak as one. "We were all chosen like you once, and all of us failed to make a choice. There is no right or wrong – you just have to make a choice. We are all half-breeds just like you. Cursed with being half and half – cursed with the choice. A choice that can only be made by one who knows what it is like to be half-human and half-Vampyrus. Choose your better half, Kiera Hudson, and you can be free."

"Free to go home?" I asked, my eyes wet with tears. "Free to go back to how it was?"

"Oh no, Kiera," one of them said. "You don't ever get to go back. This was always a one-way journey for you. The statues of your friends you see reflect the lives they will have if you choose wisely. They will lead happy lives with the people they truly love."

I thought of my friends – I thought of Potter with Sophie. Was he meant to be with her and not me? The pain inside of me was crippling when I thought of them together.

"Why me?" I begged them now. "Why was I chosen to make this choice?"

"Why are any of us chosen?" one of the Elders whispered above the sound of the weeping. "Why is anyone born? None of us chose that. It is a decision made for us. We just make the best of that choice. We don't know the answer to your question. It is a question that we have all asked ourselves. It was a question which made us fail."

"So if I choose, everything goes back to the way it was before?" I asked through my tears. "Everything gets *pushed* back?"

"Not exactly the same," one of them said. "Either Vampyrus or humans will live, but your friends will be saved. They will be just as you see them now. They will be with the people they love."

"But I love them and they love me," I said.

"They won't remember you," they said together. "You would have never touched their lives."

"Jim Murphy will only know the love that he has for his daughters, Isidor Smith, the love he has for Melody Rose, Kayla and Sam, and Sean Potter will be with his first love, Sophie Harrison. Whichever way you choose, they will either be human or Vampyrus – but they will be happy," they explained, their stitched faces staring down into mine.

"When do I make this choice?" I asked them, hoping in my heart, even though he had hurt me, that I would see Potter just one last time.

"You have already started down the path in making your choice," one of them said, but I didn't know which one.

"What path?" I asked.

"The moment you decided to find your father," they said, this time as one again.

"Was it you who left the pictures for me and Isidor?" I breathed. "Was it you who sent the letters to Sophie? Has it been you *pushing* us all in the direction we've needed to go?"

"No, that has been done by another."

"Who?"

"The one who will finally make you choose," one of them said, their voice just a whisper amongst the falling snow.

"And the other statues?" I breathed.

There was a pause, as if somehow they didn't know or weren't quite sure how to answer my question.

Then after what seemed like an eternity, they said, "What other statues?"

Confused by their answer, and pointing with my finger, I said, "These statues."

As I looked in the direction I was pointing, I gasped. There were no statues, just the graveyard, the church, and the falling snow. I looked back at the Elders and they had gone, too.

Chapter Fourteen

Potter

I sat at the end of Kayla's bed, she at the other, cradling a pillow to her chest. Her cheeks were tearstained, her green eyes dull-looking. I felt bad at seeing her so upset. She watched me, waiting for me to say something, but I didn't know where to start. It seemed like minutes were ticking by and she had only given me five. I couldn't bear the thought of her collapsing into another fit of hysterics. Could I really blame her, though?

So, saying the first thing that came into my head, I said, "I know Isidor was your brother, but he was like one to me, too."

"You had a funny way of showing it," she snapped, her anger still fresh and raw.

"I really didn't mean the stuff that I used to say to him," I tried to convince her. My excuse sounded shit and I knew it. "I was just yanking his chain, that was all."

"You did nothing but put him down," she reminded me.

"I know I did," I said, unable to look at her. "But me and Isidor made our peace before..."

"Those creatures killed him – cut his fucking head off," she hissed.

"You've got to understand, Kayla. Isidor didn't stay behind because of anything I said," I told her. "I know it might look that way."

"How else am I meant to see it?"

"He loved that girl, Melody Rose," I reminded her. "He really missed her. He had carried that picture of them until the time was right. He went and had all those tattoos done and his eyebrow piercing so he looked just like he did in that picture. He really believed he would see her again. He just got tired of waiting. He had no one for himself. Whoever left that picture for him to find was the person who killed him."

"Who left it for him?" Kayla asked, her voice softening just a little.

"I don't know," I said thoughtfully. "But someone is fucking with us, and I intend to find out who."

"You've pissed off Kiera, too," she said.

"I know," I whispered, looking down at the floor, "but I never meant to."

"For someone who doesn't intend on pissing people off, you have a really good knack of doing it," she said.

"I know," I said. "I've always been the same. But just like someone left that picture for Isidor, someone left a picture for Kiera."

"The picture of her father that I heard you talking about?"

"That's right," I said. "Someone had written that word *push* on the back, just like they had on that picture of Isidor and Melody. And just like that picture led Isidor to his death, I think the picture of Kiera and her father will lead to her death, too."

"Shouldn't you go after her then?" Kayla asked me.

"I want to, but she hates me at the moment."

"Because of that girl, Sophie?" she asked, staring at me as if I were under interrogation.

"Yes," I nodded. This time, I didn't look at the floor but straight back at her. "Despite what you or anyone else might think, I didn't sleep with Sophie. Not in this world. We used to be lovers once, but that was long before I had met Kiera and the world got *pushed* off-whack."

"Do you really love Kiera?" Kayla asked me, and for the first time since I'd met her, she didn't seem like a kid anymore, but a young woman, someone I could speak on equal terms with.

I looked at her and said, "With all my heart. I love Kiera more than I have ever loved anyone. When I saw Sophie again, I could've had sex with her. She asked me to. But I couldn't – I didn't want to. I realised I didn't love Sophie and I never really had. The love I feel for Kiera is nothing like I've ever experienced before. Okay, she drives me fucking nuts at times, as she always wants to do the right thing – but that's why I'm in love with her. She is everything I could only wish to be. She makes me a better person somehow."

"Have you told her all of this?" Kayla asked softly.

"I've told her I love her...but..."

"But not what you've just told me," Kayla cut in. "Not what really happened between you and Sophie?"

"I didn't get a chance," I said.

"Don't you think you should before you miss your chance?" she said.

"What do you mean?" I asked her.

"You said that someone is fucking with us," Kayla said, her eyes now sparkling again. "If what you say is true about that picture of Isidor and Melody, then whoever left it led my brother to his death. You said that Kiera had been left a picture of her father with that word *push* written on the back. If Kiera is walking into a trap, you might not have long to tell her how you really feel, and more importantly, save her life."

"But what is she tells me to fuck off?" I said.

"Then you'll know how we all feel every time you open that mouth of yours," she half-smiled at me.

"Am I really that bad?" I asked her.

"You're worse," she smiled. Then totally unexpected, Kayla lent forward and put her arms around me. She held me tight. "I'm sorry about what I said to you."

"You don't have to say sorry," I whispered, holding her close.

"I just needed someone to scream at and probably will again before this is all over," she said, her head resting against my shoulder. "I know deep down you thought of Isidor as your brother."

"How can you be so sure?" I whispered.

"Because you were always there for him," she said. "Whenever Isidor's back was against the wall, you risked your own life, time and time again to save his. Only a brother would do that."

I felt her body rattle against me, as she started to cry again.

"I wasn't there for him at the end though, was I?" I said, just wishing I could go back and change that. Wishing I could have been standing shoulder to shoulder with him as those berserkers came through the door. With tears stinging in the corners of my eyes again, Kayla hugged me tight.

"You saved me, Sam, and Kiera," she whispered. "You got us safely away on that train. If it hadn't have been for you, we would all be dead now. You couldn't have saved all of us, Potter."

"I should've never left him behind," I said. "I won't make that mistake again."

"Then go after Kiera," she whispered in my ear. "Go and tell her what you told me. Tell her that you love her and can't live without her. Bring her back to us. I couldn't bear to lose Kiera, too."

I eased Kayla out of my arms. Taking her face in my hands, I rubbed her tears away with my thumbs. Then, I kissed her gently on the forehead, stood up, and went to the window. Perched on the windowsill with my wings open, I looked back at her and said, "Thanks, Kayla."

"What for?"

"It doesn't matter," I said, then climbed out of the window.

Just as I was about to leap into the air, I heard Kayla say, "See you later, alligator."

With a lump in my throat, and unable to look back, I whispered, "In a while, crocodile." In my heart it didn't sound the same coming from me and not Kiera. Spreading my wings, I tore up into the sky and the snow which now fell all around me.

Chapter Fifteen

Kiera

I reached the wall of the graveyard, my legs and arms feeling stiff again. Like before, it wasn't the cold – I was cracking up – in more ways than one. Looking down at my hands, I could see that the skin had turned grey, and they were covered in tiny fractures. I touched my face with the tips of my fingers, and just like the backs of my hands, the flesh there felt broken and cracked. Without any Lot 13 or Potter to take the red stuff from, I knew that I wouldn't reach my father's house without turning to stone.

With my legs feeling like lead, I placed one in front of the other and headed towards the gate in the wall that circled the graveyard. I pushed it open, and it made a wailing noise on its rusty hinges. I looked back amongst the slanted gravestones where I had seen the statues. I didn't care what the Elders had said, apart from the statues of my friends, there had been others too. There had been that one which looked so much like me. The statue had been asking for help – but not just for me, for the others, too. My neck made a cracking noise as I faced front again, and a flurry of what looked like ash showered the front of my snow-splattered coat. It was then that I saw it. Black and long, scurrying along the edges of the wall. With what little energy I had left, I stumbled forward in the snow, my marble-looking hands reaching for the rat which crouched against the graveyard wall. I fell onto all fours and my joints cried out in pain as my knees made a cracking sound beneath me. With my chipped and broken-looking fingers, I closed them around the rat, and it squealed beneath my touch. Closing my eyes, I dug my fingers into its fleshy belly. At once, my fingers began to feel warm as the rat's blood spurted over my hands and fingers. Soon they started to soften, loosen up. Unable to open my eyes, I didn't want to see what it was I was about to do, I raised the rat to my lips. I could feel its back legs twitching and tail swishing from side to side as I sunk my fangs into it. There was a crunching sound as my teeth broke its back and I ripped a piece of its fur-covered flesh free.

As if I hadn't eaten in years, I chewed the meat up inside my mouth. The rat's bristly black fur stuck between my teeth and I gagged. I swallowed the raw lump of meat in a wash of hot, sticky blood. At once, I felt the skin around my eyes and mouth soften, like I had just gone mad with a tub of moisturiser. Keeping my eyes closed, I tore another piece of flesh from the rat which had now fallen still in my fists. Wanting to be sick, but forcing myself to not be, I chewed the tough meat between my teeth and swallowed. I could feel the rat's blood hit my stomach, and at once, my legs and arms began to feel lighter. Opening my eyes just a fraction, I looked at my hands and could see the cracks had closed over, and my skin looked soft and supple once more. I pulled the rat's head and tail from either end of its body, and stuffed what was left of the creature into my mouth. With my jaws aching from all the chewing, I swallowed the meat. My throat felt hot, as if I'd just swallowed a mug of battery acid. I cupped some fresh snow in my hands and brought it up to my mouth. It felt icy cold against my lips as I sucked some of it up and into my mouth. The snow did little to rid my mouth of the vile taste the rat meat had left behind, but it eased the burning sensation. As the snow began to melt in my hands, I used what was left to wipe away the blood that covered the outer corners of my mouth.

I knew the effects of the rat's blood wouldn't last long, and that if I were going to make it to my father's house, I would have to head for there without any further delay. Then what?

Was something going to happen when I got there? The Elders said I had to make my choice once and for all, and that I had already started along that path by deciding to find my father. What could he possibly have to do with any of this? I wondered, as I passed through the open graveyard gate and set off up the hill in the direction of my father's house.

With the snow showing no signs of easing, I cut a solitary path up the hillside. The Elders had spoken of choices, but what choice did I really have? If I didn't make my choice then, as they had already shown me, my friends and I would all end up as statues, trapped in this world. It seemed that if I did finally make my choice between the humans and the Vampyrus, then they would all go back home – to the world that they once knew. But I wouldn't be going with them. This was a one-way trip for me. I now knew that. Could I delay making my choice anymore? The effects of turning to stone were rapidly speeding up. The Lot 13 was being consumed at an ever-increasing rate by Kayla and Potter. It might last a little longer now that Isidor was no longer with us. What happened when it ran out? Did we feed off each other – draining the life from one another? Or did we do the unthinkable and start feeding from humans? That had been tried before by the Vampyrus and they had created vampires. Animals might work, but the effects wouldn't last long. What sort of existence would that be for my friends? Wasn't being dead already hell enough?

The Elders had shown me the happy lives my friends could have if I made my choice and *pushed* everything back in place. Murphy would be with his daughters – they would have never been murdered in their beds by Sparky. Isidor would be with Melody, just like he had always wanted. Kayla would have Sam and Potter would have...

To think of that was unbearable, but I had to face it. Potter would spend his life with Sophie. She wouldn't reject him in the world which would exist when I *pushed* back. Neither of them would know any different – but I would. To Potter, I would have never existed, wiped from his memory, from his life. Would I remember him? Wherever I ended up, would those feelings I had for Potter still rage inside of me? Would I spend the rest of eternity carrying the scars for the person I loved, but could never have, knowing that they were with another? Is that why the Elders carried so many scars? Why their faces and bodies seemed to be stitched back together? Were they the scars they carried for failing to make their choice? Would I become just like them – one of them?

With so many unanswered questions racing around my mind, I leant into the wind and driving snow, and continued on to my father's house. I didn't want to let any of my friends go, especially Potter. Despite my anger for him, I loved him, and nothing would ever change that. I wanted us to be happy together. I deserved that, didn't I? But that was selfish of me, right? Could I really forsake my friends; deny them a shot at happiness because of my love for Potter? I didn't want him to be with Sophie – he was mine. I loved him. I thought of those statues the Elders had shown me. The images of Murphy holding his daughters' hands haunted my soul. I remembered watching from the window at Hallowed Manor as he had carried his daughters' lifeless bodies into the woods. I could see him crying in Potter's arms as if it were only yesterday. How could I deny Murphy the chance of being with his daughters? I pushed the memories away, but they were only replaced with images of Isidor, so often alone, standing to one side, not really fitting in with the rest of us. Melody had accepted him, they had accepted each other, and the statue of them looking into each other's eyes, filled me with joy, yet sadness too. It was within my power to give them each other back, or snatch it away from them. Again, I tried to push those pictures away, but they were only replaced by images of Kayla. My sweet little sister, Kayla, who at times seemed so angry and lost, but she had a right to be – she had lost so much. Both her parents had been murdered, and so now had her brother. Kayla had found a friend in Sam; could I take him away from her, too?

Then there was Potter. Perhaps he still did love Sophie? Maybe it was Sophie he was meant to be with? The statue the Elders had shown me said so. I could carry on tricking myself that it was me Potter truly loved, but he didn't, not really. At the earliest opportunity he had gone back in search for Sophie. Could I blame him? Wasn't I now going in search of my father? I needed to see him again, to know that he was okay. Why did I want to know those things? Because I loved him. Even though I could barely imagine how painful the moment would be when I had to make my choice and send Potter back into Sophie's arms, I knew that I had to do it. I had to make that choice for Potter and for all of my friends. I loved them all enough to want to see them happy – that's all I wanted.

So with my mind set, and listening to *Iris* by Leona Lewis on my iPod, I made what was left of the short journey to my father's house. Knowing that no matter what happened there, I would be presented with some kind of choice, and I was ready to choose.

Chapter Sixteen

Potter

Within seconds, I was soaring amongst the clouds above the cottage Murphy had rented out. Did I feel bad for not explaining to him I was going in search of Kiera? Not really. It was great to have Murphy back, but for too long now, I had come accustomed to making my own decisions. Some of them had been shit, there was no denying that now, but I had done the best I could. Those were mistakes I was desperate to put right, especially the ones where Kiera was concerned.

She'd probably be really pissed at me for going after her, but I could live with that as long as she listened to what I had to say. Kayla was right; I should explain how I truly felt for her. I couldn't imagine – I didn't want to imagine – a day where Kiera wasn't a part of it. I had meant every word I had said about Kiera, when Sophie had asked me at the farm on Black Hill to describe her.

"...Kiera has this really annoying habit of wanting to do the right thing the whole time," I remembered explaining to Sophie. *"She wants to do the right thing by everyone, even if it means that she loses out somehow. She threw herself into the arms of a serial killer because she couldn't bear the thought of others suffering. Kiera is the smartest, bravest, and most selfless person I have ever known. But deep inside, she is so gentle and kind, and sometimes I think that I'm not even good enough to hold her hand, let alone share a life with her."*

To hear my own voice in my head, I wondered now if I hadn't been right about those last words I had said. To think of Kiera made me smile inside, and I knew Kayla was right. I should have told Kiera those things I thought about her. What had been the point explaining to Sophie how much Kiera meant to me? It was Kiera who needed to know how I felt about her. I just hoped that I could reach her in time – before she made it to her father's house where a trap of some kind undoubtedly waited for her. How much of a head start had she got? An hour, perhaps? She could have reached her father's house by now. I could be too late already.

With my wings angled like points on either side of me, I tucked my arms against my sides and headed in the direction I had last seen Kiera going. Snow whisked past me as it left the clouds. I dropped slightly in the air to get my bearings through a break in the clouds, and stopped. On the other side of the hill where Murphy's rented cottage stood, I could see a mass of berserkers. They were heading up the side of the hill towards the cottage where my friends sheltered. I hovered, hidden by the cloud, and watched them silently approach the cottage on all sides. They were circling the cottage to cut off any chance of my friends escaping.

I looked into the distance, wanting to go after Kiera, knowing that time was running out if I were to intercept her before she reached her father's house, and the trap I now believed had been set for her there. Below I could see the berserkers approaching the cottage, my friends unaware they were going to be attacked. I looked again in the direction Kiera had been heading, then back down at the cottage.

Which do I choose? I roared inside.

Go after Kiera and my friends would surely die. Stay and help my friends and Kiera would walk into a trap just like Isidor did. I looked back again, through the snow, hoping that I might see Kiera in the distance, on the brow of some hill. The snow perhaps slowed her progress, reluctant to use her wings for fear of being seen, therefore still visible somewhere in the distance. There was no sign of her. I looked down again as the berserkers crept around the outside of the cottage, their pointed noses sniffing in the air. With my wings spread wide on either side of me, I looked again into the distance, just hoping that I would see Kiera making her way back towards the cottage, deciding that it was a mistake to go see her father after all. There were only drifts of snow.

With my claws out, I flipped backwards in the air, and then raced out of the clouds and back towards the cottage.

Chapter Seventeen

Kiera

By the time I had reached the top of the small hill, the taste of the rat had finally left my mouth. Its blood was still working, sedating that constant need in me for the red stuff. The weather had eased a little, but the air was bitterly cold and my hair, shoulders, and coat were white with snow. At the top of the hill, the wind howled all around me, and I looked back in the direction I had come. I could see my footprints leading away into the distance and back towards the church, which now looked small, like part of a miniature town some way below me. Just like everything else, the graveyard and the spire of the church were now white, and from where I stood, the world looked peaceful, like a picture on the front of a Christmas card. From where I stood, I couldn't see any statues, and despite what the Elders had said, I knew I had seen them, and I could remember what one of them had told me.

Lead us to the Dead Waters, the statue which had resembled me had said. Even now it seemed to talk on the wind which howled about the hillside. *We will follow you.*

But where were these Dead Waters? I wondered. And what were they?

The Dead Waters will give us life, and you can't push back without us, the statue's voice had told me.

Unlike what the Elders had told me, the statue had said that if I wanted to *push* back and *save* my friends, I had to bathe in these Dead Waters. As I stood on the crest of the hill, I spied a thin column of black smoke spiralling up into the white sky. It looked like a pencil smudge on a blank piece of paper. Sheltering my eyes with my hands, I peered ahead and could see that the smoke was coming from a house in the distance. My father's house. I looked at it, then glanced back over my shoulder in the direction I had come. Did I listen to the statue and go back, lead them and my friends to these Dead Waters, wherever they me be? Or, did I continue on towards my father's house and make the choice which would ultimately set my friends free? With my head tucked down, and my long hair fanning out behind me in the wind, I set off in the direction of the house and the black spiral of smoke.

The house sat alone on an area of ground which was mostly surrounded by trees and brambles. The nearest road was about a mile or more away, which you could get to by following a narrow path which led away from the front of the house. I had been able to see this as I made my way down from the hill. Not far from the house, there was a small crop of trees. They offered some protection from the snow, as I stood and spied on the house. I'd already made up my mind; I would look at him from afar. There was a temptation, knowing my father was somewhere inside that house, to run towards it and find him. I was scared, though, now that I was here. What would it be like to see him again after all this time? I just wanted to see his face again, to know that he was all right. I could hear Murphy's and Potter's warnings inside my head, telling me that this man wasn't really my father. He was, though. It was my father in a different *when*, that was all. Now that I was so close, it was easy to push Potter's and Murphy's warnings from my mind. The desire to see my father again, and knowing that he was so close, was overwhelming.

Concealed behind the trunk of a large tree, I watched the house, hoping to see some sign of him. I knew already that my father in this *when* was slightly different from the one I had loved. My father had always liked towns. He enjoyed the convenience of it, and it was near to his work. This place was remote, unlike anything he would have usually chosen. I could see several flowerbeds lying before the house on a patch of turf. I couldn't tell if they were well-kept or not because of the blanket of snow, but I knew my father had never enjoyed gardening. Before the house stood what appeared to be crab apple and plum trees. Both were fruitless. In fact, as I stared at the house, it didn't look as tranquil and well-kept as perhaps I had first thought. Brickwork showed through, where large areas of paint had been allowed to flake away. The roof was missing some slates in several places, and the front door, which at first sight looked grey, was actually just weather-beaten and dirty. This surprised me, as my father had always been rather meticulous about how presentable and clean the house looked. Perhaps there were slight differences between *whens*? I wondered.

I rubbed my hands together, then blew warm breath over them. My fingers ached with the cold, but it was better than having them turning to stone. With my back hunched, and trying to make myself as small as possible, I peered around the edge of the tree trunk, and watched the house. The snow had almost stopped now, and I could see that no one had approached or left the house all morning by the lack of footprints leading to and from the house. I knew that my father was home by the sight of the continuous stream of smoke that poured from the chimney. He was probably sitting before the fire reading a good book. Who in their right mind, other than me, would be out eating rats and watching the house of their dead father from behind a tree?

I'd almost given up hope of seeing him, when suddenly I saw the outline of someone at the window. Was that him? I wondered. Whoever it was, they had passed the front of the window too quickly for me to see. Perhaps there was someone else in the house. A wife, perhaps? Murphy and Potter had told me that my mother had died during childbirth, but that didn't mean he hadn't remarried. Who would want to live in such a remote place on their own? Not me, nor my father – not the one I had known. How did he get to work each day? He had been a pathologist and was pretty much always on-call. Havensfield was a good five miles or more away. Was my father a pathologist in this world? Perhaps he did something completely different? Did any of that really matter? I'd only come to steal a secret look at him, not find out his life story.

I stared at the window, but there was nothing. With the sky clouding over again and the light fading, I stepped from the trees and slowly approached the house. I walked hunched over, trying to make myself as tiny as possible. I knew that I was leaving tracks in the snow behind me, but I couldn't bear waiting in the cold any longer on the off chance that my father might peer out of the window so I could sneak a glimpse of him. If the Elders had been right about what they had said, then I was meant to see my father again, and it would somehow lead to a choice that I had to make.

I stepped around the flowerbeds and approached the windows. They were arched at the top, their frames wooden and bare in places where the white paint had flaked away. Crouched beneath the windowsill, I slowly raised my head and peered through. They were dirty, and seeing through them into the room was difficult. I cupped my hands around my eyes and peered through. On the other side of the grime-smudged window, I could see a snug-looking living room. A fire roared in the hearth on the far side of the room, and there was a high-backed chair pulled up close before it. Was my father sitting in that chair, warming himself before the fire? I couldn't quite see. The back of the chair was too tall. However, to know that he could be just feet away from me felt surreal. When I had buried my father, not once did I ever imagine I would see him again. I felt sick with excitement and fear all at the same time. What if he were to suddenly stand up and look back? He would see me. How would he feel at discovering his daughter peering at him through the living room window, knowing that he had only recently buried her?

It was only as those thoughts rushed through my mind, I realised how crazy a situation I was in. Somewhere inside of me I knew that coming to see my father again had been a mistake. However much it pained me, Potter had been right. This hadn't been one of my greatest ideas. How selfish had I been? I'd only been thinking about my own grief and not my father's. What if he were to look back now and see me? It would be like seeing a ghost. He didn't have the understanding or the knowledge of what truly was going on. My father hadn't the faintest idea that the world had been *pushed*. As far as he knew, his world was still running on track – he didn't know of any other. So to see me would surely mess with his head, make him go half-crazy at the sight of his dead daughter staring at him through the window. My grief and the desire to replace those haunting memories of him, for however briefly, had blinded me.

Wishing now that I hadn't come, I crouched again beneath the window. Then, just as I was about to turn and sneak away, I heard a familiar voice and it didn't fill my heart with gladness like I had hoped – but fear.

"Kiera?" the voice said. "Kiera, is that really you?"

Slowly, I stood up, turned around and looked back at my father.

Chapter Eighteen

Potter

Knowing I had very little time to waste, I rocketed out of the sky, and headed straight for the front door. Still in flight, I shoulder-barged into it, sending the doorway flying inwards in a shower of splinters. Murphy, who I could see had been dozing in front of the fire and warming his feet, sat bolt upright. His pipe hung from the corner of his mouth as he looked agog at me.

"What the bleeding hell is going on!" he barked. Then seeing the door scattered about the room in a mass of fine splinters, he shouted, "You can fucking pay for that, Potter! I'm going to lose my deposit on this place thanks to you!"

"You're going to lose more than just your deposit any time now!" I yelled back. "We've got berserkers at one, three, six, and nine o'clock."

"Ah, just quit with all the o'clock-bollocks and speak English, can't you?" Murphy grumbled, getting slowly out of the chair.

"We're surrounded," I warned him.

"By who?" he said, fumbling for his matches in his trouser pockets.

"About twenty of those shit-faced berserkers," I told him again.

"Where?" he asked, going to the window and peering out.

Before I'd had a chance to say anything else, there was the sound of breaking glass as one giant paw shot through the window and grabbed at his face. Murphy lurched backwards, like a boxer ducking a punch.

"See!" I hissed at him.

Standing back-to-back in the room, we listened to the sound of the berserkers yapping and snarling from outside. Slowly unbuttoning his shirt, Murphy groaned and said, "You know what? I'm getting too damn old for all this shit. A man of my age should be settled down somewhere. Have a pretty wife, a nice garden and..."

"I'm sorry to piss all over your fantasy, sarge," I cut in, "but can't you just take your shirt off a little bit quicker and get your claws out?"

"Okay, okay, don't hassle me," Murphy complained. "You know I don't like to spoil my uniform. I just hate those goddamn creases you get when you just rip your shirt off and..."

"Fuck the creases!" I shouted. "Claw up right now or we're gonna die!"

No sooner had the words left my mouth when the first of the berserkers bounded through the open doorway. Almost at the same time, Sam entered the living room carrying another pot of boiling hot soup.

"What's going on?" he asked.

"What the fuck do you think?" I roared, pointing at the berserker with my claw. The creature stood up just inside the broken doorway and sniffed the air, as if momentarily distracted by the smell of the chicken soup.

"Want some of this?" Sam asked it, that crazy look suddenly back in his eyes.

The berserker looked down at him as Sam threw the burning hot soup into its face. The creature howled in pain and covered its eyes with two giant paws. Blinded by the burning soup, I lunged forward, dragging my claws across the throat of the beast. Its head rolled backwards on its neck as if attached by a lose hinge. Blood pumped from the wound in thick clots, as Kayla suddenly sprang from the top of the stairs and clung to the back of the dying creature. With her fangs glinting, she buried her face in the creature's throat and began to eat. I had become accustomed to her wild and frantic feeding sessions at the first hint of blood, but she bit and tore at the berserker with a ferocity I didn't believe I had seen her capable of before. Maybe the Lot 13 wasn't hitting the spot anymore? I wondered. After all, there wasn't anything quite like the red stuff – it was the real thing.

As the berserker staggered in a wide circle, Kayla attached to its back like a monkey, the rest of the downstairs windows blew inwards. Back-to-back, Murphy and I circled the room, swiping and biting at anything which came at us through the window.

"Just like old times," Murphy grumbled, as he lashed out at a berserker who dared to stick its snout through the window.

"You wouldn't want it any other way, you old fart," I said, burying my right claw into the eyes of a berserker which was scrambling through one of the broken windows. The creature yapped, snarled, and withdrew its head.

"We need to get to open ground," Murphy barked. "We're as good as dead if we stay in here."

I looked back over my shoulder to see Kayla and Sam in the open doorway, as they fought to hold the berserkers at bay. "Got any ideas?" I asked Murphy.

"Not really," he mumbled around the pipe which still dangled from the corner of his mouth. "You?"

The berserker that Kayla had fed from lay in a crumpled heap at my feet. Breaking away from Murphy, I hoisted it up and dragged it towards the fireplace. I laid it over the fire. It was huge and easily smothered the flames. The smell of roasting wolf flesh filled the room and funnelled up the chimney. Outside the berserkers began to howl and yap as they detected the scent of cooking meat. Now, these creatures were ferocious killers, and like all pack animals they were driven by instinct, and more often than not, hunger. The first berserker through the door had been distracted by the smell of Sam's chicken soup, so I was kind of hoping that the smell of roasting meat might just distract them some more, long enough at least for us to get out into the open. These creatures, although powerful, looked thin and gaunt, like fur-covered men that had been half-starved, and I knew that their desire to kill and hunt was driven by hunger.

Excited by the smell of the cooking meat, the berserkers yelped and barked outside. As if understanding my plan, Murphy looked at me, winked, and said, "Well done, Potter – there's hope for you yet."

I looked back at Kayla and Sam, who were still by the open doorway as they fought with their claws and fangs to keep the berserkers from getting in. The smell of the meat wafting up through the chimney and out of the front door was only driving the creatures on even more.

"Get back!" I roared at Kayla and Sam as I raced towards them, knocking them away from the door.

The berserkers seized their chance and bounded and scrambled into the room. All of them headed for the fireplace where they greedily pulled the cooking carcass from the fire. With their huge, long snouts, they pushed and shouldered each other away, keen to get at the meat. The sound of tearing meat and chewing filled the room.

"Get out of the way!" one of the berserkers suddenly screeched at another.

To learn that these creatures could actually speak made my skin turn cold.

"*Pleeeaaassee!* It was my piece," one of them whined, fighting over a scrap of half-cooked meat which had fallen from its snout and had been snatched up by another.

"Go! Go! Go!" I hissed at Kayla and Sam, pushing them out of the door. I looked back to see these half wolves, half humans driven mad by hunger and failed matching, fight each other for the meat.

Murphy sprang from the kitchen window, his slippers and shirt tucked under his arms. He dropped the slippers into the snow and wedged his feet into them and put on his white police shirt. The sergeant stripes on his shoulders glistened.

"That's better," he sighed, then walked around the side of the house again towards the dilapidated-looking barn. He returned just moments later carrying two petrol cans. "Take one of these," he said, thrusting one of the cans at me.

I watched him unscrew the lid, then splash the contents around the doorframes and window frames of the cottage.

"What you waiting for?" Murphy barked over his shoulder at me.

"What about your deposit?" I shouted over the sound of the feeding berserkers.

"Fuck the deposit," he grinned and continued to douse the cottage with petrol.

I took the cap off the can that Murphy had given me and splashed the strong, smelly petrol over the front of the house. When I had shaken the last few drops from it, Murphy looked at me.

"Stand back," he said, bending down and holding his lighter to what was left of the door frame. Within moments, greedy flames were crawling across the front of the cottage. Almost at once the heat was unbearable as the fire began to consume the building. The sound of burning wood hissing and snapping filled the air, belching plumes of black acrid smoke into the white sky.

We stood and watched the house rapidly disappear as it became engulfed by the flames and smoke. "I can hear them," Kayla said, cocking her head to one side. They're screeching and calling out for help."

"I can't hear anything," Murphy muttered, turning and heading back towards the barn and the police van.

I stood next to Kayla and Sam, and I was sure that over the sound of the roaring fire, I could hear those half human, half wolves crying and howling in fear and pain, as the flames and smoke consumed them. Then, the sounds of their cries were drowned out as the van's engine rumbled to life. The thick, black tyres crunched over the snow as Murphy drove slowly towards us.

"What are you waiting for?" he barked at us.

Silently we climbed into the van, and before I'd even the chance to slide the door shut, Murphy was heading back across the field. In the wing mirror I could see some of the berserkers run, howling and screaming from the fire, pin-wheeling their long arms in the air as they fought desperately to put out the flames that ate away at them.

Burn, you fuckers, I thought with a smile and looked away.

Chapter Nineteen

Kiera

My father looked at me through the falling snow as it settled on his jet-black hair. It was like looking at a ghost in some way, except that he was really there. It was like he hadn't died at all. When I'd last seen him, his cheeks had been sunken, his eyes like two deep holes in his face, dark-rimmed, and faded. He had been nothing more than a skeleton; even his hair had thinned and almost fallen out. I remembered his skin had looked waxy and yellow. Now as he stood before me, he looked just how I'd wanted to remember him. Handsome, full of life, his eyes sparkling blue.

"Kiera," he said sounding surprised. "What are you doing here?"

Although I had promised myself that I would only watch him from afar, to see him once again, standing so close within reach, I rushed forward and collapsed in his arms. He wrapped them around me and I sobbed uncontrollably against his chest. He smelt just how I remembered him to. Aftershave and soap. I never wanted to let go of him, I wanted to stand in that spot, as snow fell all around us, and never let go. He was my dad and I loved him with all my heart. I didn't care what anyone said, he was my dad. He looked the same, smelt the same, and held me the same. I closed my eyes against those terrible memories of him screaming out in pain as he begged the nurses for morphine. At least in this world, he would never know such agony. I wouldn't let that happen to him.

"Kiera," he whispered, pulling me close. "What's wrong?"

I looked up into his face, and could see the love he had for me in his eyes, that unconditional love that a father has for his daughter. How could I tell him, even begin to explain, that in my world he had died from cancer, and in this world – his world – I had come back from the dead?

As my mind tried to scramble into some kind of order, he said, "What are you doing here? I thought you had gone away to study for your sergeant's exam? What are you doing back already?"

I blinked and felt more of my tears trickle onto my face in warm rivulets. "I thought I was dead here?" I breathed, the words out before I had a chance to stop them.

"Dead?" he frowned. "What are you talking about?"

"I thought I was dead," was all I could say back at him, my mind now wondering if Potter and Murphy hadn't lied to me. Perhaps they had hoped if they told me my father was grieving for me in this world, then perhaps I would have left him alone – not gone looking for him.

"Well, you don't look dead to me," he smiled, brushing my fringe gently from my brow. "Come inside and warm up by the fire. I've got some of your favourite biscuits – Cadbury's chocolate fingers."

I couldn't remember ever actually liking them, but perhaps I did in this world? I wondered as he took me by the hand and led me towards the front door.

"Dad?" I said, and that word sounded strange coming from my mouth. I hadn't called anyone that for such a very long time.

"Huh?" he said, looking back at me as we reached the open front door.

"I really thought I was dead," I said, now feeling so confused that my brain was beginning to hurt.

"You're stressed, that's all that's wrong with you, Kiera," he said, leading me into the warmth. "You've been stressing about that sergeant's exam for months. I knew no good would come of it."

"But..." I started, as he closed the front door, and then took my coat from me.

"You go and sit down and warm yourself up," he said. "I'll make you a nice cup of sweet tea."

"Coffee," I whispered.

"When did you start drinking coffee?" he said with a curious stare.

"Only recently," I said, looking away.

"Coffee it is," he smiled and headed towards the kitchen.

Alone in the snug-looking living room, I armed the tears from my cheeks with the sleeve of my sweater. I sat in a chair before the fire, and glanced about the room. There were several pictures of us on the wall above the fire. I looked at them and couldn't see the picture which Potter had brought back from my flat for me. Perhaps that's why it wasn't on the wall. Thinking of Potter again, I began to feel angry at him. How dare he tell me that I was dead in this world, when I was very much alive? If Potter had been lying, then there would be two of me in this world. The other me was away studying for the police sergeant's exam.

Then suddenly standing up, realising what a mess I was creating, I headed back towards the front door. What would happen if the other Kiera – my other self – suddenly showed up here? What would happen then? My mind raced as I took my coat from the hook by the door where my father had hung it. What would happen when my other self, did return from her study leave, and my father spoke of me turning up talking about being dead?

No, I had to leave! Regardless of whether Potter had lied to me about me being dead or alive, coming here had been a big mistake. Somebody was going to get hurt, and I didn't want that someone to be my father. He had no knowledge of what had happened in the world before it got *pushed*. I was wrong to make him a part of this.

Slowly, I lifted the latch on the front door and opened it.

"Kiera?" he suddenly said from behind me.

To hear him say my name hurt so much. I never thought I would hear my dad say my name again.

"Where are you going, Kiera?" he asked sounding confused.

I daren't look back at him, because if I did, I would stay. I wouldn't be able to leave him again.

"I can't stay," I whispered, the front door half open.

"But you haven't drunk your coffee," he said gently.

"I have to go," I said, tears spilling onto my cheeks again, just wanting to turn and run into his arms.

"What's wrong, Kiera?" he hushed, coming close. "You can talk to me. I'm your dad. It doesn't matter if you fail some police exam. I'll be proud of you whatever happens, you know I love..."

"Stop," I begged him. I didn't want to hear him say that he loved me. I wasn't the Kiera he loved. I was someone else. I was a freak, a monster with claws, wings, and fangs. If he really knew what I was, he would run a hundred miles just to get away from me.

"Please just let me leave," I whispered, still unable to look back at him.

I felt him place his hand on my shoulder and pull me close. Then, unable to help myself, I turned to look at him. He had a worried look on his face. Then wrapping his arm around my shoulder, he said, "Don't look so sad, Kiera. You look so pretty when you smile."

Looking into his eyes, I smiled back at him. Then, there was a sudden flash of light. With my father's arm wrapped about my shoulders and the smile still on my lips, I turned towards the light. In the open doorway stood a hooded figure, a camera in its hand.

Chapter Twenty

Potter

"Stop the van," I told Murphy.

"Are you out of your tiny fucking mind?" he barked at me.

"I'm going after Kiera," I told him as he raced the van through the maze of winding country roads.

"I only came back because I saw those berserkers…" I started.

"What do you mean, you only came back because you saw the berserkers?" he glanced at me as he navigated the narrow roads.

Sam and Kayla sat quietly in the back of the van.

"I was on my way to find Kiera," I explained. "I think she is walking into a trap."

"You don't know that for sure?" Murphy said. "And even if you are right, who do think is behind it?"

"How the fuck should I know?" I said. "Whoever has been screwing with us since we came back, I guess. And besides, we promised we would wait for her at that cottage until tomorrow morning, and you've just gone and burnt it down."

"So did you!" Murphy reminded me.

"Look, I'm not interested in who set fire to the goddamn cottage," I said. "I just want to go and get Kiera."

"Then we go together," Murphy said, slamming on the brakes so hard and fast that I shot from my seat. My face smashed into the windscreen and I roared in pain.

"Can you stop doing that!" I yelled. "Every time I get into a vehicle with you, I end up with a broken fucking nose"

"Quit complaining, you tart," Murphy grunted as he tried to turn the van in the road. "Jesus, you're meant to be this superhuman creature from the underworld, and you're sitting there bitching because you've bumped your head!"

"Bumped my head!" I roared in disbelief. "You just about smashed my face in." Then touching the end of the nose with the tips of my fingers I said, "Look, I've got a nosebleed now thanks to you."

"Let's have a look," Kayla said sticking her face between the front seats and sounding hungry.

"Fuck off, Kayla," I snapped at her. "I've just stood and watched you eat a berserker, for crying-out-loud. Now, sit back and get a grip, for fuck's sake!"

"You're such a grouch," she moaned, taking her seat in the back again.

"I just want to go and get Kiera," I groaned.

"We're going," Murphy barked at me. "Stop getting so excited."

"I'm not getting excited!" I seethed.

"Yeah you are," Sam said from the back of the van.

I glared at him over my shoulder and said, "Who asked you?"

"I just think that those berserkers were not just after us because of what happened at Ravenwood School," Sam started to explain. "Nor do I think they are just after Kiera because they suspect she is this dead angel who has come to destroy the wolves."

"What you trying to tell us, kid?" Murphy said, glancing up so he could see Sam's reflection in the rear-view mirror.

"Those berserkers and the Skin-walkers want Kayla, too," he said.

I turned again in my seat and looked at him. "What are you talking about?"

Sam glanced at Kayla, then back at me, as Murphy listened but concentrated on driving the van. "When that wolf tried to match with me back at Ravenwood School," he started to explain. "It was like I got a glimpse into the wolf's mind before Isidor saved me. I could hear its thoughts – its feelings. Me and Kayla had both been chosen for matching. Kayla had been chosen because McCain had kept reports on all of the kids there. He made reports about Kayla – detailed reports. He noticed that she was different in some way to the others. The wolfman can look human but his intended bride, a wolf named Lola, was meant to have matched with Kayla. But you showed up with Kiera and Isidor and we all managed to escape. The wolfman is still looking for Kayla – he wants her to be his bride."

"Did you know about this?" Murphy asked, glancing back at Kayla.

She sat quietly and nodded.

"Why didn't you say anything?" I asked her, not feeling angry but confused.

"Because there seemed to be so much going on," she started. "What, with us needing to get Sam to the Fountain of Souls."

"Fountain of Souls?" Murphy spluttered.

"You've heard of it?" Sam asked him.

"Heard of it?" Murphy barked. "I died there."

"Is that were the wolves killed you?" Sam said.

"One of your kind double-crossed him and ended up ripping his heart out," I barked at Sam.

"Well, we have to go back," Sam said, staring back at me.

"Why?" Murphy asked, cocking an eyebrow at him in the rear-view mirror.

"Because that's where the Dead Waters are," he said.

"The what?" I asked straight back.

"I don't know exactly, but the wolf who tried to match with me knew about them. He had been warned about them," Sam said. "I know they can help you."

"How?" I pushed.

"I've seen you all drinking from those little bottles that you carry around in your pockets," he said, looking at each of us in turn. "I know about the cracks that form in your flesh. You look like you're turning to stone unless you drink that pink stuff in those bottles or feed off each other."

"How do you know about that?" I asked, feeling suddenly suspicious of him again.

"He saw me start to turn to stone at Ravenwood," Kayla spoke up. "He stabbed me and the wound started to turn to stone, just like a statue. Sam gave me some of the Lot 13 I had smuggled into the school with me."

"He stabbed you?" I snapped, my suspicions growing ever stronger.

"It's a long story," Kayla said. "It was a mistake, that's all. But you should listen to Sam."

"We can't go back to the Fountain of Souls," I said, looking sideways "That's where the wolves live. How do we know he's not leading us into a trap just like we were led into one before by the Lycanthrope?"

Murphy didn't answer straight away. He sat and stared at the road ahead, through the snow which had started to fall again. "Go and find Kiera, Potter," he finally said.

"What about you?" I asked him.

"I'm going to take Kayla and Sam back to the Fountain of Souls and see if I can't find these Dead Waters," he said.

"Are you for fucking real?" I said. "Have you forgotten what happened there?"

"I can't forget," Murphy said. "But what other options do we have? Drive around with our thumbs up our arse until the lot 13 runs out, until we've bled each other dry and we all turn to stone?"

"Kiera was taking us to the fountains," Sam cut in.

"No one asked you," I snapped back at him. Then, looking back at Murphy, I said, "Are you sure about this?"

"I've heard that the fountains and the caves beneath them have been vacated by the wolves in this world," Murphy said, glancing at me. "Perhaps the boy is right."

"We've put our trust in a wolf before," I tried to remind him again.

Murphy slowed the vehicle and pulled into a snow-laden ditch. "We'll wait for you on the edges of the forests which conceal the fountains," he said, looking at me. "Now don't just sit there admiring my good looks. Get going and bring Kiera back safely. If what the kid says is true about these Dead Waters, it could be the answer to our prayers."

Without saying another word, I climbed from the van and stepped onto the road. Murphy started the engine again, and slowly drove the van away. I patted my coat pocket and listened for that reassuring clink of the bottles of Lot 13. I thought I'd hidden the fact that I'd too been cracking up, from everyone – even Kiera, who always saw everything. But I hadn't fooled the boy, Sam. He had seen and knew a lot.

I watched the van disappear around a bend in the road. Then, when I was alone, I opened one of those tiny bottles, threw my head back and gulped down the gloopy pink substance in one large gulp.

Chapter Twenty-One

Kiera

"Who was that?" I gasped, the sudden flash from the camera causing me to blink. When I opened my eyes again, the hooded figure had gone from the open doorway and I wondered if it had even been there.

"Oh, they just wanted to take our photograph," my father smiled at me.

"Sorry?" I said, feeling utterly confused. "Who wanted to take our photograph?"

"Pay them no mind," he smiled, reaching out behind me and swinging the front door closed.

The wind howled outside as I thought of the photograph which Potter had brought back from my flat. I looked at my father and realised *that* photograph had just been taken as he stood with his arm around my shoulders. I looked at his jet-black hair and realised that the white streaks of grey I had seen in the photograph hadn't been his fading hair at all, but the last flakes of melting snow carried in on his hair from outside.

"Dad, we are in danger," I breathed. "We can't stay here."

"What are you talking about, Kiera?" he frowned.

"Someone has set a trap for us," I said, reaching for the latch.

"A trap, for me?" he frowned again, but this time I was sure I could see the faintest traces of a smile tugging at the corner of his lips.

"No," I said, sensing that something was suddenly very wrong here. "A trap has been set for me."

"Very good," he said, suddenly pulling me close. He snaked his arms around me, but it wasn't like the hold of a father

– more like that of a lover. He ran one hand through my hair, and the other down my spine letting it come to rest in the small of my back.

"What are you doing?" I squirmed against him, feeling scared and uncomfortable. "Let go of me."

"But I'm your father," he whispered, his lips curling upwards, making his face look suddenly unkind. "I'm your *daddy*."

His hand, which was still in the small of my back, slowly slid further down and I felt his fingers brush over my buttocks.

"Get off me!" I screeched, pushing him away with the palms of my hands. "What are you doing?"

With his arm wrapped so tight around me I was beginning to find it difficult to breathe, my father looked into my eyes. Their almost perfect blue began to fade and take on a new colour. A brighter colour. Yellow. His eyes almost seem to spin in their sockets and sink further back into his face. Again I tried to pull away, but he held onto me. Just like his eye sockets had begun to form to dark hollows in his face, his cheeks began to sink inwards too. At first I thought that somehow, he was being eaten up by the cancer again. That the two worlds were overlapping. Then, as he pulled me closer, so the tips of our noses were almost touching, his face began to ripple – twist out of shape, until it looked like someone I recognised.

"Jack Seth!" I gasped, feeling repulsed by his touch.

He gave me a knowing smile, his lips rolling back to reveal his black rotting gums and broken teeth. His face looked more emaciated than I had remembered it to be. His thin, wispy hair stuck out from the sides of his head and from behind his ears. Just as his face had changed, so had his body. It stretched against me, and again I tried to pull away from him. His bony arms were locked around me like a vice. I looked up into his face as he towered over me. I no longer felt scared, just angry and confused.

"Why? I asked him.

Before he had the chance to answer, I heard the front door swing open behind me, a flurry of snow sweeping in and making me shiver in Seth's arms.

I glanced back to see that hooded figure standing in the open doorway again. It was difficult to see if it were male or female. With face hidden and body concealed beneath long, grey robes, there was nothing for me to *see*. Glancing back at Seth, I stared into his eyes. I tried not to, but it was hard to resist. His eyes spun around and around like two Catherine wheels in their sunken sockets.

"What do you want with me?" I breathed, no longer revolted by his touch.

"I want you to choose," he smiled.

I felt a sudden pain in the back of my head and everything went black.

Chapter Twenty-Two

Potter

I didn't know if Murphy had made the right decision in heading for the Fountain of Souls and the Dead Waters that Sam had spoken of. Murphy was a law unto himself on most occasions. I knew there had been little point in trying to get him to change his mind. Time was precious now if I were to stop Kiera walking into the trap I believed had been set for her. Maybe I was being paranoid? Perhaps she would just take a peek at her father had head back to the cottage again? I doubted that. The picture of Kiera and her father suggested something different – that something was very wrong.

With the wind pulling my hair from my brow and my wings flapping like two giant sheets that had been hung out to dry, I soared through the air and towards Kiera's father's house. I prayed that I wasn't too late. How much precious time I had wasted going back to help my friends, I didn't know, but what else could I have done? It was a choice that I had to make. I just hoped that it hadn't been the wrong one. All I wanted was to get Kiera back. I didn't want to waste any more time in finding her. I needed to tell her what I really felt. I would tell her everything, and why I had kept secrets from her. It hadn't been because I'd wanted to cheat or deceive her somehow – it had been because I loved her – wanted to protect her. If she listened and believed everything I had to say, I wanted to ask her something. I wanted to know if and when we *pushed* the world back to how it had been before, if she would spend the rest of her life with me? There was no one I wanted more than Kiera. I had known that for some time – probably since our first kiss in the gatehouse back at Hallowed Manor. Even though I'd been wearing that stupid fucking disguise – another one of Murphy's great ideas – that kiss had been very real to me. It had felt like no other kiss I had known.

Kayla had been right. This was the sort of shit I should have told Kiera – not kept it to myself. Just like those letters I had sent to Sophie after she had rejected me, I should have perhaps written down how I felt and given it to Kiera to read, if I hadn't found the courage to tell her myself. Why hadn't I done that? Because if I were to be really honest with myself, I was scared that Kiera would have ultimately rejected me just like Sophie had. She wasn't Sophie, though – she was *Kiera Hudson* and that made her something very special.

I dropped altitude and swooped through the clouds to get my bearings. I sensed that I wasn't too far away from Kiera's father's house. Careful to remain hidden, I arched my wings back and slowed. Hovering, I peered through the breaks in the cloud cover. Below was a vast sea of white fields which stretched in all directions as far as the eye could see. It was almost impossible for me to find a landmark to aim for. Then, in the distance I saw something reaching up into the sky. It was a church spire. I raced towards it.

Within a matter of seconds I was above the church and looking down at the desolate graveyard. The world seemed so quiet, like I was the only person living. It was like the snow had smothered any sound, other than the wind which howled all around me. Then, looking to my right, I could see a pinprick of black and it was moving across the fields towards what looked like a barn. I shot forward through the cloud to get a better look. It was a person, head down, trudging through the snow. With wings poised, I swooped closer, the black speck of colour moving across the snow becoming clearer. I screwed up my eyes against the falling snow, not quite believing what I was seeing. I flew closer still, dropping out of the clouds, praying that my eyes weren't deceiving me. The solitary figure drew closer as I swooped overhead. I couldn't see their face, as they walked almost bent over against the driving snow. I didn't need to see the face to know who it was. It was Kiera. I sighed with relief to know she was still alive.

Chapter Twenty-Three

Potter

Kiera lifted her head and looked at me through the falling snow. It covered her hair and the shoulders of her coat. Not everything was pure white though. I could see a smear of blood about the corner of her mouth. Blood dripped from her fingers and splattered the snow.

"Kiera, are you hurt?" I asked, taking a step towards her.

"What are you doing here?" she asked, her eyes fixed on mine. Her voice sounded resentful.

I stopped. "I came after you," I said.

"So you could gloat and make a few more wise-arse comments?" she asked.

"No, I came after you because I was worried about you," I said, daring to take another step closer.

She looked at me, her hair hanging wet and bedraggled against her pale face. "Well, you'll be pleased to know you were right," she said.

"Right?" I asked her. "Right about what?"

"It was a trap," she said, looking at me, her eyes full of pain and distrust.

I just wanted to go to her and hold her in my arms. I didn't. "A trap?" I asked her. "Set by who?"

"Jack Seth," she said back. "It was Seth who sent your letters to Sophie. He also left those pictures for Isidor and me."

Hearing that it was Jack Seth who had been screwing with us filled me with a burning rage. To know that he had led Isidor to his death and had deceived Kiera made me want to rip his fucking head clean off. "Where is he?" I snapped at her.

"He's dead," Kiera whispered. Then, looking down at her hands, which still dripped blood into the snow, she added, "I killed him."

"Where?" I asked, going towards her.

"At my father's house," she said, looking back into my eyes. "My father wasn't there. There was only Jack. He boasted of what he had done. I was so angry, Potter. I ripped his throat out."

"Are you okay?" I asked, finally taking her in my arms and holding her against my chest.

"I guess," she whispered against me.

"I'm so sorry," I said, holding her tight in the snow. "I never meant to hurt you, Kiera," I told her. "I'm sorry I kept secrets from you."

"It's over now," she said, pulling away from me.

"What is?" I asked, trying to take hold of one of her blood-stained hands. She pulled away.

"We're over," she said, looking back at me. "I thought I could trust you. But you lied to me, Potter. I've been lied to before. I'm not going there again."

"Let me explain," I said.

"What's the point?" she shrugged, looking at me.

"Because I love you, Kiera. I love you more than anyone or anything," I tried to convince her.

"And what about Sophie?" she asked me, knocking snow from her fringe with the back of her hand.

"Fuck Sophie," I said back.

"And I guess that's what you did when you went to find her again," Kiera said, holding my stare, as if wanting to see my reaction to her accusation.

"I never did," I wanted to shout. I didn't though, I kept my voice calm. I didn't want to argue with her.

"So what did you do together?" she asked.

"Let's talk before we go back," I said, taking her by the arm.

"Where?"

"In that barn over there," I said, nodding in the direction of the barn I had seen from above. "We can keep out of the snow and the cold while I explain everything to you."

"You've got five minutes," she said, looking at me.

"You're the second person to have said that to me today," I half-smiled at her.

"Who was the first?" she asked, as I led her through the snow towards the barn.

"Kayla," I said back.

I pulled the barn door open, and the smell of old animal feed and hay wafted under my nose. It didn't smell too bad, although I guessed that if Isidor was still with us, he would be covering his nose and mouth and choking. It wasn't the greatest of places, but it had a roof, and bales of comfortable-looking hay were piled in the corners. I closed the door and led Kiera towards the hay. I reached up and took two bales from the pile. With my claw, I sliced apart the rope which secured them. I scattered the hay over the ground, making an area which was soft, warm, and comfortable for us to sit on.

I sat down and looked up at Kiera. "Gonna join me?"

Pulling her coat tight about her frame, she sat down on the hay a foot or so away from me. I took a pack of cigarettes from my pocket and lit one of them.

"Do you really think you should be smoking in a barn?" she asked. "What, with all the hay?"

Any other time, I would have continued to smoke regardless. Today, I crushed the cigarette between my thumb and forefinger and put it out.

"So?" she asked.

I looked at her.

"Your five minutes are running out," she reminded me.

Knowing that I had very little time to waste, I looked at her and said, "I love you."

"Do you?" she asked right back.

"Yes," I said, my mind trying to remember exactly what it was that I had said to Kayla. I had expressed my feelings well back then, but now sitting with Kiera, my mouth went dry and I couldn't think of the right words.

"You have a funny way of showing it," Kiera said, still staring at me. "I know you used to love *her*."

"I thought I did once," I tried to explain, my mouth feeling sticky and dry. "But after meeting you, I knew that the feelings I had for her were nothing compared to how I feel about you. It's you I want."

"How do I know you are telling the truth?" she pushed.

"Look, I'm not very good with words," I said, inching towards her and taking her hand in mine. This time, Kiera didn't pull away. I wiped the blood from the back of her hand. Then, very slowly, I lifted it to my mouth and gently kissed it. Her hand felt cold. I placed it against my cheek. "I love you so much," I told her. "Would I have come looking for you if I didn't? I might not be good with saying how I feel, but doesn't the fact I am here now with you and not her, show you how much I love you?"

Kiera slowly cupped my face in the hand which I had pressed to my cheek and looked into my eyes. Then, very slowly, she leant forward and kissed me. Folding my arms about her, I kissed her right back.

Chapter Twenty-Four

Kiera

I opened my eyes. The back of my head hurt from where I had been struck. I tried to lift my hand to touch the lump which I could feel throbbing, but my hands wouldn't move, they were strapped behind me. I lifted my head, and could see I had been tied to a chair. My feet were fastened with chains at the ankles. I was in a dimly-lit room. The only light was the pale winter rays that streamed through a filthy window set into the wall. I knew I was upstairs in my father's house somewhere, as when I looked through the window, all I could see was sky and the tops of the trees in the distance. The floorboards were bare and made of wood. They looked rough and splintered. The room smelt of mildew and damp. Green wallpaper had once covered the walls, but it now hung in long pale strips, like flesh which had been peeled from a bone. Opposite me sat another person, but I couldn't see who it was as they were covered in a grey coloured blanket. The wind roared around the eaves and the windows rattled in their woodworm infested frames.

"Let me out of here!" I screamed, struggling to break free.

From behind me, I heard the sound of chuckling. It was dry and rasping. I glanced back over my shoulder to see Jack Seth step from the shadows, as if he had been part of the wall itself.

"Release me, Seth!" I screamed at him, his crazy yellow eyes glowing from the two deep holes in his face.

"I don't think so," he smiled, coming to stand in front of me.

Strapped to my chair, he towered over me like a giant stick insect. His body was so painfully thin, I wondered how it managed to keep him upright. He was dressed in a denim shirt and jeans, a baseball cap perched on his head. A red coloured bandanna was tied about his scrawny throat.

"Why are you doing this?" I cried, and again I yanked against my restraints. A bolt of pain splintered up my arms and across my shoulder blades as I tried to pull my hands free of the chains.

"Why am I doing this?" he said, kneeling down so he was staring straight into my face. "Because you failed to make your choice."

"You said that back at Hallowed Manor," I said. "That's why you tricked me into believing McCain was a killer. The Treaty has failed because of what happened to McCain. Isn't that enough?"

"No, no, no!" he smiled, wagging one long finger from side to side just inches from my face. "I won't be happy until I've repaid you for what you did to me in The Hollows. I want to see the great Kiera Hudson make a choice."

"But I have," I shouted at him. "The Treaty failed because of me. I chose not to save McCain."

"That wasn't a real choice," he smiled, but behind it I could see a wall of rage. "Not like the choice you were chosen to make by the Elders in The Hollows. You could have set me free, Kiera Hudson, but you didn't. You used me because you were so fucking weak. Because you couldn't decide between the humans and the Vampyrus, you punished me!"

As he spoke, his smile faded into a grimace and his voice got angrier. Then standing, he stood in the middle of the room. "I helped you, and that's how you repaid me."

"You didn't help me," I shouted back at him. "You just helped yourself!"

"I saved you and your friends' lives!" he roared, spit flying from his face and splashing the dried-out floorboards.

"Your back was against the wall in The Hollows. The half-breeds and Vampyrus had beaten you. You were outnumbered, outwitted and out-fucking-classed. If it hadn't have been for me leading the Lycanthrope to help you, you and your friends would have all been dead."

"Don't stand there like some kinda freaking martyr!" I yelled at him. "You only saved me to save yourself. You needed me to lead you to the Dust Palace and the Elders, so they would lift your curse."

"And they were so close in doing so when you had to go and throw yourself at me!" he screamed, his fist clenching in and out, and the tendons on his neck pulsing beneath his wrinkled flesh.

"You didn't have to kill me!" I roared at him. "Just like me, you had a choice."

"I didn't have a choice," he screeched at me. "That's the curse. The moment you threw yourself into my arms – the moment you offered yourself to me, I had to kill you. I had to take you. I didn't have a choice. Why can't you understand that?"

"I wasn't talking about that choice, you piece of shit!" I screeched back at him, my hair falling over my face. "I'm talking about the choices you and your race made before you were cursed. I'm talking about the reason you were cursed. You didn't have to go around raping and killing children and woman. You chose to do that, and that's why you were doomed to live as Lycanthrope."

"I can't be blamed for the choices my ancestors made, you stupid bitch," he spat. "I was cursed before I was even born."

"That's no excuse," I shouted back. "We all have a choice – that's what separates us from animals."

"So at last the great Kiera Hudson agrees that we all have a choice to make!" Then leaning in close to me again, the tips of our noses touching, he hissed, "So why did you fail to make yours?"

I looked into his crazy eyes, and again I saw us together in them. Me and him as lovers. I looked away.

"Like what you see?" he whispered into my ear. "Turn you on, does it? Want a piece of little old Jack, do you?"

"Go fuck yourself," I spat, fighting the urge to look into his eyes again.

"You were so sweet," he said, pressing his nose into my cheek as if sniffing my flesh.

"It doesn't take much of a man to rape a corpse," I hissed, the smell of his breath turning my stomach.

The side of my face exploded in pain as Seth drove his fist into my cheek. There was a cracking sound as my head snapped to the side under the weight of his blow. "You were very much alive and enjoying every minute of it," he whispered in my ear. "You *loved* me."

"I know what true love is," I whispered back into his ear. "You have no idea what that is like."

Seth pulled away and stood up. He looked down at me, a smile forming on his thin, bloodless lips. "You speak of Potter, don't you?"

I ignored him and looked away.

"Potter! Potter! Potter!" he said, clapping his hands together. "What a silly little bitch you really are. The great Kiera Hudson who can *see* all." Then, leaning close again, he smiled and said, "You don't see shit, little lady."

"I *see* enough," I said back.

Then, reaching into the breast pocket of his denim shirt he said, "I want you to see this. I want you to see what your beloved Potter is really all about."

Seth thrust an iPod under my nose. I saw the crescent-shaped moon logo, then looked away.

"Frightened of what you might *see*?" Seth taunted me. "Told you about Sophie, did he?"

"Yes," I nodded, not wanting to give him the satisfaction of thinking Potter had kept secrets from me. "They used to be lovers – he told me that."

"Did he tell you that he went looking for her as soon as he came back to this world?" Seth teased.

"Yes," I whispered.

"Did he tell you what fun they had?"

"He told me she was dead," I said.

"Before that?" he pushed.

"I don't care," I lied, and he knew it.

Seth chuckled, making that sound again, as if he were choking on straw. "Did he tell you why he killed Eloisa?"

To hear her name, I couldn't help but turn to face Seth again.

"Potter didn't tell you why he ripped her heart out, did he?" he smiled just inches from my face.

"He told me he killed her because she was a child killer," I breathed, feeling sick.

"I'm supposed to be a child killer and he didn't rip my heart out, did he?" Seth said, and this time he didn't smile, he looked intently at me.

"What other reason could there be?" I asked him, fearing that I already knew the true reason in my heart.

"Because they had been lovers," he said softly. "Potter was scared you might find out that he had had sex with her. He didn't want to destroy the illusion he had created for you."

"You lie," I whispered, but all the while remembering how Eloisa had always seemed to hang around Potter in the town of Wasp Water. I tried to push the memories I had of seeing them together away, but I couldn't. As if those light bulbs were popping inside my head again, I saw...

...Potter leaning against the custody block wall. Eloisa towered behind him, her perfectly shaped legs seeming to go on forever in a pair of tight-fitting jeans. Her long, blond hair spilled over her shoulders and down the front of the black jacket she wore. Her skin was pale, but this only highlighted her blood-red lips and golden eyes. I couldn't help but notice how close she stood beside him, and I didn't like it.

"Good to see you back in the world of the living, sweet-cheeks," he said, coming towards me.

When he was close enough, I rolled my arm back, then punched him straight in the face.

His head rocked back on his neck, and the cigarette which had dangled from the corner of his mouth span away. "What was that for!" he snapped. "I've been trying to save you!"

Then, gently touching Potter on the shoulder, Eloisa said in the sickliest sweetest voice that I'd ever heard, "Sean, I'll go and find Jack, you two look as if you need to talk." Then she was gone, striding away on those damn legs of hers.

"Sean!" I hissed. "No one ever calls you Sean!"

"It's my name," he snapped back.

Those memories I had of Potter and Eloisa at the police station flashed brightly inside my head. I closed my eyes, screwing them shut, hoping they would go away. The bulbs of light inside my mind popped and flashed as if blinding me. In them I saw me and Potter standing alone in the police station at Wasp Water...

... "What's gotten into me?" Potter scoffed. "If I remember rightly, you smacked me in the face the moment you laid eyes on me!"

"Where do you get off on making decisions for me without even asking?" I roared.

"What decisions?" he shouted back.

"Deciding that I'm to go off hand in hand into The Hollows with that killer, while you go off to rescue Luke with that walking pair of breasts on legs!" I hissed.

"Breasts on legs?" Potter said, nearly choking on a throat full of cigarette smoke as he stifled his laughter. "You mean Eloisa? You're jealous and that's what this is all really about," Potter smiled. "You're pissed because I've been spending time with her."

"Oh, please," I groaned, "Why don't you take your head from out of your own arse and...

...In those flashes of light I saw Potter lean in to kiss me, but then at the last moment, before our lips had met, he turned, as if to look at another. Lights flashed inside my mind and...

... Without saying a word, Potter walked directly towards Eloisa. She smiled at him and her eyes twinkled. Potter's face looked grim and his eyes a dull black. Then, so quick if I'd blinked I would have missed it, Potter shot his arm out and thrust his claw into Eloisa's chest. It all happened so fast that Eloisa still had that smile on her face as Potter ripped out her heart. She looked at him as if to say something, but all that came out of her mouth was a thick jet of black blood. Eloisa fell forward, crashing face first onto the floor of the hangar...

...I felt my face being slapped. I opened my eyes to see Jack Seth staring at me.

"You remember, don't you," he breathed into my face, and I recoiled at the stench of his hot breath. "You are *seeing*, aren't you? You know what I say is true. Your beloved Potter and Eloisa were lovers."

"You lie," I said, feeling sick and faint. "It's not true."

"Did Potter ever tell you what happened at the Wolf House?" he smiled at me.

"The Wolf House?" I asked, feeling numb and confused.

"Of course he didn't," Seth said. "Why would he? Because that's where Eloisa and Potter first met. Where they first had sex together. How happy he must have been when the gorgeous Eloisa walked back into his life. And where were you when that happened? In a fucking zoo – being treated like an animal. Why didn't Potter come and rescue you like he promised? Because he was too busy fu..."

"Shut your face!" I shouted at him, not wanting to hear any more. If my hands were free I would have covered my ears so as not to hear what he said. Deep inside of me I remembered asking Potter why he hadn't come to save me from that zoo...

... *"Now I can see why you took so long in coming to find me!" I shouted. "You were living it up with her!"*

"Her?" Potter said, looking now somewhat bemused. "Eloisa, you mean? She's not so bad."

"Well you've definitely changed your tune," I spat. "Only a few weeks ago you were babbling on about how you could barely forgive a girl for having hairy armpits let alone a hairy tongue!"

...How had I been so blind? I screamed inside. Seth had been right – I hadn't *seen* shit. If Seth had been right about that, was he also right about what he had told me about Potter and Sophie?

"You know I'm telling you the truth," he said. "You feel it in your heart."

"I don't have a heart," I whispered back.

"And neither can Potter for hurting you like this," Seth said, his voice now sounding as if he actually cared for me. "But still he hurts you and you just don't see it, Kiera Hudson."

"What do you mean?" I said, lifting my head to look at him.

"Look," he said, holding up the iPod for me to see. "Again, you are trapped and in pain, desperate for the help of the man you love. But just like Potter left you in that zoo so he could be with another, he once again betrays you."

"With who?" I breathed looking at the little flat screen which had been set to face time.

"Take a look," Jack sighed with a smile.

Chapter Twenty-Five

Kiera

The screen flickered into life. I could see what looked like an empty barn. Whoever was filming the scene was doing so covertly and was hidden. The door to the barn swung open and I saw Potter. Someone followed him inside. The light was poor, and at first I couldn't see who it was. They were female. I watched in silence as Potter went to a stack of hay, reached up and took two bales of hay which he scattered on the floor to make what looked like some kind of bed.

The woman stepped closer into view, and my skin turned cold. Potter sat on the hay, then reaching out, he asked Elizabeth Clarke to sit down next to him. I looked up at Seth.

"What's he doing with that school teacher?" I gasped. "She's a friend of yours isn't she? A wolf."

"And don't we now know that Potter likes himself a piece of wolf," he smiled back at me.

"But why would he..." I started.

"Shhh," Jack hushed. "Let's see if I'm right about Potter." I looked back at the iPod.

"I love you," I heard Potter tell Elizabeth, her golden hair hanging wetly about her shoulders.

"Do you?" she asked him.

"Yes," Potter said, and I thought I was going to be sick again as I heard him say that to her. Is that what he had said to all of us? Eloisa, Sophie, and me?

"You have a funny way of showing it. I know you used to love her," Elizabeth said.

Was she talking about me? I wondered.

"I thought I did once, but after meeting you, I knew that the feelings I had for her were nothing compared to how I feel about you. It's you I want," I heard Potter tell her.

However much it crushed me inside, I knew he was talking about me. God, he was good. "Turn it off," I snapped at Seth.

"Watch," he insisted.

With tears beginning to blur my vision I looked back at the screen.

"How do I know you are telling the truth?" I heard Elizabeth ask him, her lips covered in bright red lipstick.

"Look, I'm not very good with words," Potter told her. Then I watched with tears streaming down my face as he reached out and took Elizabeth's hand. He kissed it, and then pressed it against his cheek. *"I love you so much,"* Potter told Elizabeth.

"Please turn it off," I cried, turning my head away. I couldn't bear to watch any more.

Then gripping my face in his bony hands, Seth roughly snapped my head around and forced me to look at the iPod. "Look," he barked. "Look and see that I am telling the truth."

I watched as Elizabeth cupped Potter's face in her hands, then slowly lent forward and kissed him on the lips with her perfectly formed mouth. Potter kissed her right back. He ran his fingers through her long white-blond hair, laying her down in the hay. I wept silently as he positioned himself on top of her, his hands slowly pulling free her wet clothes. Elizabeth responded, by pulling at his coat.

"Turn it off!" I screamed. I couldn't bear to watch anymore. I couldn't bear to watch the man I loved make love to another woman.

"Watch!" Seth screeched, waving the iPod in front of my face.

I glanced at the iPod long enough to see Potter was now naked to the waist, as was Elizabeth. Potter had one of her ample breasts cupped in his hand.

"Turn it off," I sobbed, pulling my face free of Seth's grasp and looking away. "I believe you. *I believe you.* I don't need to see any more."

Seth switched off the iPod and threw it to the floor.

"Why did you have to show me that?" I wept, knowing I would never be able to rid myself of those images. Each time they appeared in my mind, they would only reinforce the hatred I now felt for Potter.

"You would only be able to make your choice if you fully understood the truth," Seth said.

"What choice!" I screamed at him, dribble and snot swinging from my chin.

"Who are you going to choose?" Seth smiled back at me. "Because only one of them can live."

"Who are you talking about?" I cried, just wishing this torture would come to an end already.

"Are you going to choose Potter, the man you now know is a cheat and a liar and has no real love for anyone other than himself, or..." Seth trailed off.

"Or who?" I breathed.

"Your father," Seth beamed, pulling back the blanket which covered the figure sitting in the chair on the opposite side of the room.

Chapter Twenty-Six

Potter

I pulled Kiera's wet coat free as she yanked mine from over my shoulders and down my back. She kissed my face and I kissed back, covering her cheeks and forehead. With her nails, she pulled my shirt open down the front and kissed my chest. Her lips felt soft against me and my flesh tightened, covered with gooseflesh. It wasn't the cold that made me shiver, but the excited feelings I felt at being with her again. My shirt fluttered to the ground, and with my claws I pulled open the front of her shirt and covered her breasts in kisses. She groaned beneath me and arched her back so I could pull her shirt free from beneath her.

"I love you, Kiera." I whispered, sliding my knee between her legs and pushing them apart.

"I love you, too," she whispered back, her fingers fumbling with my belt buckle.

I looked down at her beautiful face as she stared up into my eyes, and in the gloom of the barn, they shone yellow, not hazel. I cupped one of her breasts in my hand, and kissed her neck. Her skin smelt sweet, like perfume, and my phantom heart raced. My fangs nipped the flesh just behind her ear and she moaned softly. I didn't want to feed yet, I didn't want our lovemaking to be over – not just yet. Slowly, I covered her breasts with soft kisses, working my mouth down over the flat of her stomach. With my free hand, I popped open the top button of her trousers. She lifted her butt off the mattress of hay so I could free them. Lying on the hay in just her panties, I looked down at her beautiful body. Her skin was a cream white and soft. I slowly moved my fingertips around the curve of her hips, and she shuddered.

"I'm glad you've given me another chance," I whispered, lowering myself over her. "I have Kayla to thank."

"Kayla?" she groaned.

"I told her how much I loved you, and she said I should be telling you, and not her," I said, stroking the hair from her brow so I could see into her eyes.

"Good," she smiled up at me, her eyes shining.

"It almost broke my heart to hear her say, 'see you later alligator'; it just wasn't the same," I whispered, kissing her neck.

"Why was that?" she murmured, running her hands through my hair, then down across my back.

"Because you weren't there to say the other part," I told her, making circular motions with my fingers around the nipple of her left breast.

"The last part?" she sighed, looking at me through half-opened eyes.

"Yeah you know...In a while..." I started.

Kiera slowly opened her eyes and looked at me, and there was a blankness in them, as if she didn't know what I was talking about.

"Say the last part," I said, looking down at her, my hand now hovering just over her breast.

"Stop playing these games, Potter, and make love to me," she said, squirming seductively beneath me and gripping my arse with both hands.

"You don't know the last part, do you?" I said.

Kiera snapped open her eyes and looked up at me.

"In a while crocodile," I whispered plunging my fist into her chest.

Her eyes bulged in their sockets and her mouth snapped open as I ripped her heart from her chest. As it beat in my blood-soaked claw, Kiera's face began to change beneath me. It twisted and stretched like putty, taking on a whole new shape. Her black hair lightened before my eyes, turning from black to blonde.

"You fucking wolves just don't learn, do you?" I roared, looking down into Elizabeth's dead face. *"Fuck!"* I screamed, jumping up and throwing her still-beating heart at the barn wall where it stuck momentarily, then slid to the floor. I watched it travel down the wall like some vast black coloured slug, a trail of sticky hot blood behind it.

"Fuck!" I roared again, kicking out at her corpse, knowing that I had been tricked again. Just when I thought I'd gone and got things straightened out, I go and find that I've been humping a freaking wolf! How the fuck was I going to explain this little episode away, I did not know.

What the fuck is Kiera going to think if she ever found out? I screamed inside, kicking the wolf's dead body again. It skidded across the hay-covered floor, then rolled over.

I thought of how Eloisa had tricked me into believing I had been with Sophie at the Wolf House, by blinding me with her eyes. Elizabeth Clarke had just done the same thing to me.

"Why do I keep falling for this shit?" I roared out loud, snatching up my shirt. I'd wasted enough time already. The fact that I had been tricked like this, and by one of Seth's accomplices, told me I had been right after all. A trap had been set for Kiera, and Jack Seth was the one who had set it.

Chapter Twenty-Seven

Kiera

I looked across the room at my father. He sat just like I was, bound to a wooden chair. Unlike me, he had been stripped, wearing just a pair of boxer shorts. A leather gag had been secured in his mouth. His eyes bulged in their sockets with fear.

"Aaaarrrgghh!" he said, trying to speak from the other side of the gag. He shook his head from side to side and looked at me.

"Let him go!" I shouted at Seth.

"Only you have the power to do that," Seth smiled at me, revealing his broken stumps for teeth.

"Aaaarrrgghh!" my father groaned again, his eyes now streaming tears onto his cheeks as he stared across the room at me.

"What are you trying to say?" Seth smiled into his face.

"Aaaarrrgghh!" my father came again, shaking his head frantically from side to side.

"Perhaps I should remove this?" he said, untying the gag at the back of my father's head.

"Kiera!" he spluttered as soon as the gag was free. "Kiera I'm so sorry. I didn't get a chance to warn you. They arrived just before you got back from your study leave."

I looked across the room at him, wondering if I were truly dead in this world or not? Potter and Murphy had said that I was.

"I'm dead, aren't I?" I said looking back at him, his half-naked body tied to the chair.

Before my father had a chance to say anything back,

Seth came across the room towards me, and placed his sunken cheek against mine.

"Shhh!" he hushed into my ear. "You are dead here. Your body lies in the graveyard at the foot of the hill. You were shot in the line of duty – very sad it was too." Then, leaning back from me, he looked at me with his crazy yellow eyes and said, "Of course he doesn't remember that now. I stared at him and he sees something different now – he *sees* that you are very much alive, the memory of your death erased from his mind."

"You bastard," I whispered, looking back at Seth.

"No – not a bastard. How I wish I was, but that is another story," he smiled back at me.

"I'm not your daughter," I shouted over Seth's shoulder at my father. "I'm not really your Kiera. He is tricking you."

"Kiera, what are you saying?" my father said from across the room, his pale face full of fear. "I don't think pretending you aren't my daughter is going to help us."

"I'm *not* your daughter," I tried to convince him. "Your daughter – your Kiera - is *dead!*"

"Oh this is going to be so much fun," Seth chuckled, clapping his hands together.

"What have you done to my daughter?" my father shouted at Seth. "Why have you got her to say these things?"

"Oh please stop," Seth cried with laughter. "You're killing me."

"You've got to listen to me," I shouted at my father over the sound of Seth's laughter. "He wants you to believe I'm your daughter, because whatever this twisted fuck has planned, only works if you believe I'm your daughter."

"Kiera," my father gasped. "I've never heard you use such language before."

"Please stop," Seth shrieked with enjoyment, wiping tears from his eyes. "Please, I can't take anymore. He is actually telling you off for swearing like any decent father would. Oh Christ, this is amazing. I love it. Love it!"

I pulled again at my restraints, just wanting to be free so I could tear his face off. "Just let us go!" I roared at him.

Wiping the last of his tears away, Seth looked at me, and still trying to contain his laughter, he said, "That's a choice only you can make, Kiera Hudson."

"What choice?" I yelled at him. "What are you talking about?"

"Okay, okay," Seth said, finally getting to grips with his fit of hysterics. Then kneeling before me, his back to my father, he lowered his voice and said, "We both know that isn't really your father, right?"

"Right," I whispered looking over his shoulder at my father, and in my heart knowing it really was, but just in a different time – a different *when*. He was the same man, and the sight of him tied petrified looking to that chair crushed me.

"We both know that the man you love – Potter – will make his way here. He won't be able to resist. When he does, he will die. Simple. The only way you will stop that from happening, is if you warn him in some way, or you stand shoulder to shoulder when he arrives and defend him. It's still very unlikely that he will survive, but the odds will be better stacked in his favour with you beside him. But the thing is, and this is the real trick, you won't be able to warn or help Potter if you are a statue."

"What are you talking about?" I snapped, pretending I had no idea what he was going on about.

"Kiera, you know what I'm talking about," he smiled at me, his voice still just a whisper. "I can see the faint lines – cracks – forming around your eyes and mouth. Before very much more time has passed, your flesh, your body will start to crack and peel, just like a statue. How will you help your beloved Potter then?"

"You don't really think you will..." I started, but Seth just smiled back at me like a crazy.

"But does Potter really deserve your help – your undying love?" he teased. "After all, we know he would fuck anything with a pulse." Then looking me up and down, he added, "Or not."

"Don't judge everyone by your own disgusting standards," I hissed back at him.

Ignoring my remark, Jack Seth continued. "But to stop yourself from turning to stone, you need flesh and blood. Now, if I'm not mistaken, I can only see one place where you are going to get some of that around here," and he glanced back over his shoulder at my father.

"You evil, fucking..." I started, finally understanding the true horror of the trap Seth had set for me. "I'm not going to eat..."

"Why not?" Seth cut in. "What difference does it make if you eat him? After all, it's not as if he is your father. You've just told him you're not his daughter."

"You can't do this!" I roared at him as he stood up before me. "I'd rather die than eat..."

"That is a choice you are free to make," Seth grinned at me. "But then so will your father and Potter. I really couldn't give a shit either way."

"You won't get away with this!" I screamed at him. "Potter will be here soon and will rip your fucking heart out!"

"Potter won't be here for a good few hours yet," he smiled. "I will make sure of that. No, no, no, there is still plenty of time to make your choice."

"I won't choose," I spat at him.

"That's up to you," Seth said, heading back towards my

father. "But don't be too hasty in making up your mind. Those cravings I know you have will become unbearable before long, your flesh with start to harden. But I will stay with you, Kiera, I won't leave your side. Because once you start to turn hard and cold, how will you get across the room to feed if you choose to save Potter over your father?"

"I won't choose," I said, staring at my father. "You won't get me to choose between my father and Potter."

"So you are his daughter then?" Seth quickly said, seizing on what I had just said.

"Kiera, you are my daughter," my father said, his eyes wide in fear. "And I love you. Don't worry – help will come – you just wait and see."

I felt like screaming in agony at the choice Seth had given me. How could I choose? Even though Potter had cheated and lied to me, I couldn't let him walk blindly into a trap and to his death. But I wouldn't feed off my father to stop that from happening. If I didn't get any of the red stuff, I would turn into a statue and be unable to help either of them.

The burning sensation in my throat and stomach was already there, reminding me that before long I would need blood again, if I were to stop myself from cracking up. The effects of the rat were already fading. I stared back across the room at my father. He looked scared and helpless. Only I could save him. I thought of Potter in Elizabeth's arms. I saw him with Sophie and Eloisa, and I felt sick.

"So who will it be?" Seth asked, as if being able to read my mind.

I just stared back across the room at him.

"Perhaps you need a little something to help you make up your mind," Seth smiled back at me, his eyes spinning wildly.

Then, turning to face my father, he slowly dragged one

of his long broken fingernails across his chest. At once my father screamed in pain, throwing his head back and fighting against his restraints. Seth's fingernail peeled away a strip of my father's flesh, and I couldn't help but think of how a scoop rolls back the top layer of ice-cream in a tub. Except this lump of ice cream was flesh coloured, blood-red, and covered in wiry black chest hair.

With my father's eyes bulging from their sockets, he screeched in pain. The sound was horrendous and gut-wrenching. I pulled my hands against the chains that held them, just wanting to cover my ears and block out the sounds of his agony.

"Stop!" I screamed. *"Please stop! I can't bear it."*

"Only you can stop this, Kiera," Jack suddenly screamed back, a thick strip of my father's chest hanging from his hooked fingernail. He came slowly towards me.

I looked past him and at my father. He was slumped forward, his chest heaving up and down as he sucked in lungfuls of air. Blood ran from the opening in his chest. The Vampyrus part of me wanted to leap from my chair and feed from him. The human part wanted to go and hold him in my arms, and tell him everything was going to be okay, that I would save him from this hell.

Seth stopped before me, the strip of my father's flesh swinging from his fingers like a bloody pendulum. I snapped my head away, the smell of the blood making that feeling in my stomach burn with hunger.

Seth let the end of the strip of flesh touch my forehead. He then slowly, so very slowly, drew it down over my face, over the tip of my nose, then against my mouth. The flesh felt hot against my lips. I closed my eyes, fighting the horrific urge to snap open my mouth and swallow it whole. Seth continued to dangle the meat just over my lips.

"Hungry?" he whispered, over the sound of my father screaming out in pain behind him.

I opened my eyes and looked into his. "I'd rather die," I whispered.

Jack smiled down at me. "Your choice," he whispered.

Chapter Twenty-Eight

Potter

I stood over Elizabeth's corpse, and watched it slowly change back into the wolf which had hidden just beneath the surface of the human she had once matched with. I briefly wondered what the true human had been like, what they might have become if they had never been matched with the wolf? What had the real Elizabeth Clarke been like? Did I give a shit? Not really.

I kicked the wolf out of anger and frustration at being cheated by one of them again. Then, from behind me I heard a noise. I span round, claws out in front of me. I scanned the barn. The noise came again, like something moving behind the pile of bales to my right. I slowly moved towards the sound. The bales of hay were stacked high above, and I glanced up just in time to see them topple down onto me. I fell backwards, and as I did I saw a quick flash of movement behind them. I sprang to my feet, claws poised, and headed towards the back of the barn. Another quick flash of movement, this time to my left. I span around to find the Oompa-Loompa kid standing amongst the bales of hay. His face looked twisted and burnt, just as I had remembered it to be at Hallowed Manor. His nose looked as if it had been melted away, leaving two puncture wounds in the centre of his face. His mouth looked as if it had been pulled into a permanent grimace. He wore the Ravenwood School blazer, shirt, and tie I had seen him in before. To be honest, he looked kind of creepy.

"Dorsey, isn't it?" I asked him.

He didn't reply. I watched him place what looked like an iPod into his blazer pocket.

"Been listening to some tunes?" I asked, wondering where he had come from and if he had been watching me and the wolf make out.

"You killed my mother," Dorsey suddenly screeched, launching himself through the air at me. As he hurtled towards me, hair sprouted from his face and hands, which now looked like razor-sharp claws. In that moment before he clattered into me, I couldn't help but see the resemblance between Dorsey and Sam. For someone so small, he was incredibly strong, lifting me off my feet and throwing me into the back wall of the barn. The wooden planks splintered and snapped as I crashed into them. With my wings unfolding from my back in a blink of an eye, I sprang back across the barn towards him.

"Don't make me kill you!" I roared. "I ain't into killing no kids."

Closing my claws into a fist so as not to slice open his skin, I hit him squarely in the chest. He shot back and upwards into the wooden beams which spanned the roof. Dust showered down like rain from above and covered me. Dorsey clung to one of the beams with his claws and pulled himself up. I watched as he bounded along and over the beams high above with the grace of a hound. His long, dark hair billowed out behind him as he howled in rage. Then, dropping like a stone, he leapt down at me. His claws ripped through my shirt, tearing three long gashes in my chest. As I breathed, my lungs felt as if they were on fire. Dorsey spun around on the hay-covered floor and readied himself to pounce again. His mouth was open, and his gums were swollen with a mass of jagged teeth.

"Here, boy!" I barked, lunging myself at him. With my arms pin-wheeling on either side of me, I slashed through his blazer and flesh, sending up a spray of blood. The wolf-boy yelped in pain, his claws scraping across the ground. "Don't make me kill you," I warned him again.

Ignoring me, Dorsey sprang into the air again. I ducked, skidding away across the floor. I looked up to see Dorsey bound back off the side of the barn and come racing towards me. With my back hunched, I crouched low and thrust one of my claws out before me like a set of knives. The wolf-boy was coming at me too fast to slow down. I felt my claws slice into his belly as he became skewered on my fist. He looked at me in shock and surprise. A thick stream of blood ran from the corner of his mouth.

"Why did you make me kill you?" I whispered, slowly withdrawing my claw from within him. He shook violently, and I caught him.

With his head resting in the crook of my elbow, I looked down into his face as he twitched in my arms. His bright yellow eyes began to fade, and turn a pale blue. His burnt flesh changed, too. It kind of smoothed out, unwrinkled before me, revealing a handsome-looking boy of about twelve. Where his burnt skull had once been bald, blond hair started to show through. It was the same colour as Elizabeth's – his mother's. I looked down at the small schoolboy I cradled in my arms.

"Why did you have to fight with me?" I whispered.

Closing his eyes, he whispered, "The nightmare is over for me now, thank you." Coughing up a clot of blood, he twitched once more in my arms, and then fell still. I could feel something pressing against my leg, from within his blazer pocket. I searched inside and removed an iPod. I looked at the small crescent-shaped moon logo on the back and thought of Kiera.

"Kiera!" I breathed, placing the iPod into my coat pocket.

Then, just as I was about to let the dead boy slide from my arms, there was a burst of white light. I looked up to see a hooded figure standing in the open doorway of the barn, holding up a camera.

"What the fuck?" I said, my eyes still partially blinded by the flash of white light.

I blinked, desperately trying to focus. When I looked again, the hooded figure was standing before me. A pair of bright yellow eyes, burnt from within the darkness beneath the hood.

Fixing me with its eyes, the hooded figure whispered, "Where is Kayla Hunt?"

I tried to resist the bright yellow eyes from beneath the hood as they locked onto mine. I knew where Murphy, Kayla, and Sam were heading, and I felt like screaming it over and over again. I fought not to. I tried to look away, to break that stare, but I couldn't.

"Where is Kayla Hunt?" the hooded figure whispered again, bright yellow eyes spinning round and around.

"The Dead Waters," I whispered back.

"Thank you," the hooded figure said, the brightness now fading in their eyes.

I shook my head from side to side, as if just waking from a deep sleep. "Thank you for what?" I breathed.

"The photograph," the hooded figure whispered, turning and heading back towards the barn door where a snarling pack of berserkers now stood.

"The photograph?" I whispered, then looked down to see I was still holding the dead wolf-boy in my arms.

Gently, I placed him on the floor, before I was roughly dragged out of the barn and into the snow by the berserkers. They outnumbered me; there were too many for me to fight and possibly win. There were several Skin-walkers too, hidden by their human skins and disguised as cops. Before I knew what had happened, I felt a blow to the small of my back. I cried out and dropped to my knees in the snow.

The berserkers howled and yelped with a feverish excitement as another kicked me in the face. For the second time that day, I felt blood gush from my nose. I collapsed forward in a heap, the snow turning red with my own blood, as the berserkers and Skin-walkers set about beating me to a bloody pulp.

"Jack doesn't want him dead," one then woofed, as if reminding the others. "This one is going to be put on trial for the murder of the boy and his mother."

As I felt the right side of my head cave in under the boot of one of the Skin-walkers, I knew they had the evidence to put me on trial, as they had that photograph. I placed my hands over my head to protect myself from the never-ending rain of blows. I knew now that Kiera had walked into a trap just like I had. I hoped she was doing better than me. Knowing Kiera, she probably was. Peering through my blood-soaked fingers, I could see what looked like several statues standing alone in the field. Their heads were tilted back, arms raised in the air. I knew they hadn't been there before. I closed my eyes, shutting out them and the pain.

Chapter Twenty-Nine

Kiera

Seth took the strip of my father's flesh away from my lips. Part of me wanted to lunge for it. My stomach cramped, and I could feel the skin around my eyes and lips start to harden and crack. Seth tilted his head back, and opening his mouth, he sucked down the stringy lump of flesh like a length of spaghetti.

He smacked his lips together, and looking at me, he said, "Shame to waste it."

"You disgust me," I hissed at him.

"Really?" he smiled. "You won't be saying that in a few hours, you'll be begging me for some of your father's hide."

"Never," I snapped. "You just don't get it, do you?"

"Tell me," he smiled, heading back to my father, who sat slumped forward in his chair, delirious with pain. "What is it I don't understand?"

"I did make a choice back in The Hollows," I hissed. "I chose not to choose. No one can make me do anything I don't want to do. That's what choice is all about. That's what freedom is all about. But you wouldn't understand that."

Seth didn't say anything back. Instead, he entwined his twig-thin fingers into my father's hair and yanked his head back. Then looking at me, he slowly drew one of his fingernails around the outside of my father's right eye. My father closed his eyes, tears running down his cheeks, as he murmured, "Please. Not my eyes. *Please.*"

Above the sound of his desperate pleas, I heard what sounded like running water. I looked at my father and could see a dark patch growing on the front of his boxer shorts, and a thin stream of urine running down the inside of his leg.

"Oops!" Seth grinned.

"Leave him alone!" I roared, again fighting against the chains which fastened me to the chair.

"Why?" Seth barked back. "He means nothing to you. You said he wasn't your father."

"He is my dad!" I screamed back. "Please let him go. He has nothing to do with this. It's me you hate. It's me you want to *punish.*"

"Kiera," my father sobbed in pain and fear.

"You can end this right now," Seth roared back. "Choose between your father and Potter!"

"I can't," I sobbed, lowering my head. "Please, can't you just stop this?"

"Which is it to be?" Seth pushed.

I heard my father scream out in pain like a wild animal. Seth was raking his long, jagged fingernails across my father's stomach. His flesh came away in bloody strips.

"Who do you choose?" Seth roared over the sound of my father's deafening screams.

I thought of Potter, and despite what I knew, what Seth had showed me, I couldn't deny the feelings I had for him. However much he had hurt me, lied and deceived me, I couldn't let him walk into a this trap. In my mind all I could see was his cranky smile, that obnoxious look I so often wanted to wipe from his face, and hear the cocky remarks that spewed from his mouth. I thought of all the times we had made love, and a part of me couldn't believe that none of those feelings had been real. However much I thought I hated him, I didn't. I loved him, and had since that first time he had winked at me and called me "Tiger" back in The Ragged Cove. I couldn't give him up.

"Who do you choose?" Seth roared at me again, over the cries of my father.

I looked across the room, and just wanted to be held by

him again, just like we had so often done before. I remembered the nights, as a child, sat on his lap while he read fairy tales to me. I could see him sitting by my bed, soothing my nightmares away. I could see myself holding his skeletal hand as he cried out in pain, begging for painkillers as the cancer slowly ate him up, piece by piece. As I now stared at his tortured face, tied to the chair, his flesh being slowly peeled from him, I couldn't rid my mind of those memories of my father in his hospital bed, screaming in pain.

"Stop it!" I shrieked, just wishing I could block out my father's screams.

"Who do you choose?" Seth screamed back.

"Please," I sobbed, dropping my head again. *"I beg you."* Then, looking at the floor, feeling the chains around my wrists and ankles, and the sensation of my skin starting to crack, I could *see* something – something I hadn't seen before.

Slowly, I raised my head. I looked across the room at Jack Seth and matching his stare, I said with the upmost defiance, "My name is Kiera Hudson – who are *you* to make me choose?"

In my heart, I had made my choice. The only way I would save Potter *and* my father, was if I became a statue.

'Dead Seth'

(Kiera Hudson Series 2)
Book 5
Now Available

More books by Tim O'Rourke

Vampire Shift (Kiera Hudson Series 1) Book 1
Vampire Wake (Kiera Hudson Series 1) Book 2
Vampire Hunt (Kiera Hudson Series 1) Book 3
Vampire Breed (Kiera Hudson Series 1) Book 4
Wolf House (Kiera Hudson Series 1) Book 4.5
Vampire Hollows (Kiera Hudson Series 1) Book 5
Dead Flesh (Kiera Hudson Series 2) Book 1
Dead Night (Kiera Hudson Series 2) Book 1.5
Dead Angels (Kiera Hudson Series 2) Book 2
Dead Statues (Kiera Hudson Series 2) Book 3
Dead Seth (Kiera Hudson Series 2) Book 4
Dead Wolf (Kiera Hudson Series 2) Book 5
Dead Water (Kiera Hudson Series 2) Book 6
Witch (A Sydney Hart Novel)
Black Hill Farm (Book 1)
Black Hill Farm: Andy's Diary (Book 2)
Moonlight (Moon Trilogy) Book 1
Moonbeam (Moon Trilogy) Book 2
Vampire Seeker (Samantha Carter Series) Book 1

Printed in Great Britain
by Amazon